"I never said I didn't *desire* you," Dylan said in a low, rich voice that practically oozed testosterone.

He was acting like their madcap embrace was a good thing. Emily fumed. "How dare you!"

He stepped forward and further invaded her space. "How dare *you*?"

With effort, Emily ignored the sexual tremors starting deep inside her. Determined to get command of a situation that was fast escalating out of control, she extended her index finger and tapped him on the center of his rock-solid chest. "Let's get something straight, cowboy." She waited until she was certain she had his full attention. "My request for help did not include anything sexual."

He winked at her facetiously. "Too bad, 'cause if it had, I might have said yes."

Dear Reader,

The best thing about being single is the independence. The freedom to do what you want, when you want, without answering to anyone. The nicest aspect to family and friends is the emotional connection. Knowing that there is someone there for you whenever, however you need them.

For many of us, the dilemma then becomes how to forge and maintain ties without losing either our autonomy or the liberty we cherish.

Emily McCabe would like to settle down one day, if she can find the kind of enduring love her parents, Shane and Greta McCabe *(A Cowboy's Woman)*, discovered in their wildly improper marriage of convenience years before. The only problem is she doesn't want anyone telling her what to do, and the one man...the only man...she has her eye on thinks she needs "taming"!

Dylan Reeves has zero interest in marriage and, in fact, has sworn he will never be tamed by any woman. What Emily doesn't know is that the lonesome horse whisperer has an incredibly kind heart and would be so much happier if he just belonged to a big family, like hers.

Obviously, they have nothing in common. Which is what makes him the perfect candidate for the pretend boyfriend she needs. The only question is, what will it take to make the very sexy Dylan Reeves say yes to her outlandish proposal?

Happy reading!

Cathy Gillen Thacker

One Wild Cowboy

CATHY GILLEN THACKER

TORONTO NEW YORK LONDON
AMSTERDAM PARIS SYDNEY HAMBURG
STOCKHOLM ATHENS TOKYO MILAN MADRID
PRAGUE WARSAW BUDAPEST AUCKLAND

Recycling programs
for this product may
not exist in your area.

ISBN-13: 978-0-373-75354-3

ONE WILD COWBOY

Copyright © 2011 by Cathy Gillen Thacker

All rights reserved. Except for use in any review, the reproduction or
utilization of this work in whole or in part in any form by any electronic,
mechanical or other means, now known or hereafter invented, including
xerography, photocopying and recording, or in any information storage
or retrieval system, is forbidden without the written permission of the
publisher, Harlequin Enterprises Limited, 225 Duncan Mill Road,
Don Mills, Ontario M3B 3K9, Canada.

This is a work of fiction. Names, characters, places and incidents are
either the product of the author's imagination or are used fictitiously,
and any resemblance to actual persons, living or dead, business
establishments, events or locales is entirely coincidental.

This edition published by arrangement with Harlequin Books S.A.

For questions and comments about the quality of this book
please contact us at Customer_eCare@Harlequin.ca.

® and TM are trademarks of the publisher. Trademarks indicated with
® are registered in the United States Patent and Trademark Office, the
Canadian Trade Marks Office and in other countries.

www.eHarlequin.com

Printed in U.S.A.

ABOUT THE AUTHOR

Cathy Gillen Thacker is married and a mother of three. She and her husband spent eighteen years in Texas and now reside in North Carolina. Her mysteries, romantic comedies and heartwarming family stories have made numerous appearances on bestseller lists, but her best reward, she says, is knowing one of her books made someone's day a little brighter. A popular Harlequin Books author for many years, she loves telling passionate stories with happy endings, and thinks nothing beats a good romance and a hot cup of tea! You can visit Cathy's website at www.cathygillenthacker.com for more information on her upcoming and previously published books, recipes and a list of her favorite things.

Books by Cathy Gillen Thacker

that was before Mom figured out who you *should* be seeing," Hank explained.

Emily's heart sank.

She had no doubt her mother meant well, too.

Thanks to more than thirty-six years of happily wedded bliss with the love of her life, there was no one more romantic than her mother. Her father, in his own way, was just as bad although her dad had yet to actually approve of any man she'd dated.

"Tell me you're pulling my leg here," Emily pleaded.

"Nope." Jeb flashed a grin. "Mom's planning to play matchmaker at tonight's charity dinner for the Libertyville Boys Ranch."

There was no way Emily could avoid the fund-raiser. Her Daybreak Café was one of a handful of restaurants in town providing food and beverage for the outdoor event. Plus, it was a worthy cause.

Emily picked up the reins and bridle while Hank carried the saddle and blanket to the tack room. She put the riding equipment away, then turned back to face her brothers. She swept off her flat-brimmed hat and slapped it impatiently against her thigh. "Surely Dad isn't going to sign on for this foolhardiness."

If there was anyone who could talk sense into Greta McCabe, it was her husband….

Her three brothers watched as she went to the fridge in the corner and took out a bottle of blackberry-flavored water, kept on hand just for her.

"Actually," Holden recounted, serious as ever, "Dad thinks Mom might be onto something. You have to admit, you have been one heck of a bum magnet on your own."

Emily narrowed her eyes. "Thanks, heaps."

Jeb chuckled. "It's true, little sis. Who knew there were so many losers in the world till you dragged them all home?"

Emily recalled with startling clarity why she'd had such a hard time with her love life. Part of it was her ability to see the "potential" in just about everyone. The only problem was, most men did not want to be "improved" and certainly not by the woman they were dating. So she constantly had to shelve her need to help. The rest had to do with the fact that all the truly successful men she had met seemed to want a woman who'd be content to tend to *their* needs and live in their shadow. Few wanted a woman who was already successful in her own right.

But not wanting to get into any of that with her brothers, she turned to the third and most annoying reason her love life remained a bust.

"My lack of dates this past year is because no guy in his right mind has wanted to come near me knowing he would have to put up with you-all constantly breathing down our necks."

Hank refused to apologize. "We were just trying to protect you."

Emily glared at her three tall, brawny brothers. "Well, stop!"

Holden looked her in the eye and held the line. "No can do. Now, here's the plan. We're sure we know better than Mom and Dad who you should be dating. So…we have each picked out a guy for you to meet. All of them understand the restaurant business—so you should have something in common—and all of them already get along with us." He smiled confidently. "And as a bonus, none of them are from around here. So it won't be anyone you've already met and rejected."

Emily didn't care where these potential suitors hailed from. "I'm not going on any blind dates!" she warned. "And especially not with any men that have already received the McCabe

Men Stamp of Approval!" That would simply confirm they were the type who would bore her to tears.

Jeb grinned, mischievous as ever. "That's the beauty of our plan, baby sis. You won't have to go out with them, 'cause we're bringing them to you at the cafe. You can scope them out while you're serving them breakfast or lunch and then decide who you want to go out with—and then we'll set it up for you."

This was insane, Emily thought. Like some sort of reality show she never would have signed up for in a million years. "These three guys agreed to be looked over by me, like hunks of prime beefcake?"

For the first time, her brothers looked uncertain. Aha, Emily thought, this plan did have a hitch! And a possibly insurmountable one, at that...

Grimacing, Holden said, "They all agreed to have breakfast or lunch with us at your place. The meals themselves are going to be more like business meetings, with a little socializing thrown in."

"And during said meeting, I'm supposed to come over, make nice and flirt a little," Emily mused sarcastically.

Jeb shrugged and regarded her as if she were overreacting. "Couldn't hurt."

Oh, yeah? Emily drained the rest of her water in a single gulp and tossed the empty bottle in the recycling bin. "You're making it oh so tempting," she drawled in her Scarlett O'Hara imitation, batting her eyelashes for effect, "but no. Besides, I already have a date," she fibbed with as much bravado as she could muster. "It's tonight, at the benefit for the boys ranch, as a matter of fact. So you might want to pass that on to Mom and Dad, because I know they wouldn't want to interfere in a date I already lined up."

"Is that right?" Hank prodded, clearly not believing a word of what she'd just said. "With whom?"

Emily mentally ran down the list of eligible men in Laramie, Texas, and quickly centered on the one who would be the least desirable, at least by her family's standards. The one man who had sworn he would never be tamed by any woman…

She beamed at them proudly. "Dylan Reeves."

"No."

Emily stared at the sexy rancher in front of her, sure she hadn't heard right. Especially, since she had just offered the town's most notorious bachelor the kind of deal he couldn't possibly resist. "No?" she repeated, stunned.

Dylan Reeves swept off his hat, ran an impatient hand through his thick, wheat-colored hair and stepped out of the round training pen. His golden brown eyes lasered into hers with disturbing accuracy. "That's what I said."

Emily cast a glance behind Dylan at the once-wild gelding who was now mooning after his momentarily distracted trainer like a little puppy awaiting his return. Then she returned her attention to the ruggedly fit cowboy who was scowling down at her.

Dylan wasn't just an incredibly attractive man with a towering build that dwarfed her own five-foot-seven frame. He was a horse whisperer who had moved to Laramie five years before and, through sheer grit and hard work, founded the Last Chance Ranch.

Dylan took on the horses everyone else had given up on, and transformed them.

That being the case, Emily reasoned, he had a heart in there somewhere that would allow him to participate in yet another worthy cause. "It's a fund-raiser for charity."

His lips formed an uncompromising line. "It could be a dinner for the Crown Prince of England for all I care." He lounged against the metal rails of the round training pen and folded his arms in front of him. "The answer is still no."

Emily ignored the way the tan twill shirt hugged his broad shoulders and molded to the sculpted muscles of his chest before disappearing into the waistband of his worn, dark blue denim jeans. She forced her gaze away from the engraved silver-and-gold buckle on his belt. "Look. You know we have nothing in common," she said as a shimmer of awareness shifted through her, "so there's no possibility this will be a real date. That's why I asked you to go with me tonight."

Dylan narrowed his eyes at her. "*Asked* being the operative word. You asked…I declined. As, I might point out, I have every right to do. End of story."

"Fine." Emily stepped closer and tilted her head toward him. "Then what's it going to take?"

He looked her up and down suspiciously, from the top of her flat-brimmed hat, to the toes of her favorite burgundy rattlesnake boots. "What do you mean?"

"How many free meals at the café?" she bartered.

Initially, she'd thought two was fair. Evidently not, in his opinion.

Dylan flashed her a crocodile smile that didn't begin to reach his life-weary eyes. He rubbed his jaw with the palm of his hand. "What makes you think I want to eat at your restaurant?"

"Oh," Emily looked him up and down just as impudently and mocked his condescending tone to a T. "Perhaps the fact that you're there every morning when I open—and sometimes lunch, as well. And you've asked more than once why I don't serve dinner at night!"

That alone conveyed that either he couldn't cook, or he was too unmotivated to do so. He also had a penchant for the cowboy cuisine she had perfected.

Poking the brim of his cowboy hat up with maddening nonchalance, he leaned toward her and whispered conspiratorially, "It's a good point, sweetheart. You'd make more money if you did stay open through the dinner hour."

She would also be competing with her mother's restaurant, which was a Laramie institution and had a dance floor and lively music every night.

"I would also have to work much longer hours," Emily replied, suddenly flustered by his blatant nearness.

He smirked in a way meant to infuriate. "Or—" he prodded "—hire more staff."

Emily harrumphed. The last thing she wanted was anyone telling her how to run the restaurant she had dreamed up and started from scratch. "I don't want to hire more employees. I like my café the way it is—open for breakfast and lunch six days a week. Now," she said, peering at him sternly, "back to what we were saying...."

Dylan chuckled and released a long-suffering sigh. "Goodbye, I hope?"

She ignored his stab at a joke and stepped even closer, not caring that the move left mere inches of empty space between them. She felt the heat emanating off him, stronger and warmer than the April sunshine overhead. "Just tell me your price, cowboy." *To keep me from being thoroughly humiliated in the wake of my premature claim to have a date with you.*

Emily stood and propped both hands on her hips. "How many meals is it going to take for you to pretend to be my date for the evening? I need you just long enough to scare away the man my parents have picked out for me—and to disabuse my brothers of their own lame-brained matchmaking idea."

"None." Dylan gave her a steady look, then straightened and moved behind her. Taking her by the shoulders, he pivoted her in the direction of her car. As abruptly as he'd taken hold of her, he dropped his firm but gentle grip and stepped away. Her shoulders tingled as badly as the rest of her. "'Cause I don't do family drama," he said flatly.

Temper boiling, Emily whirled back around to face him.

He lifted one work-roughened palm. "And I don't tame women, either."

Tame! Had he actually used the word *tame?* "Excuse me?" she fumed, daring him to say that again!

The corners of his lips twitched in barely checked amusement. "Your family is right. You are a woman in need of 'assistance' when it comes to dealing with the opposite sex." He paused, wearing a self-assured, faintly baiting expression, then returned to the pen and the magnificent horse he'd been training when she arrived.

He closed the gate behind him and let his glance drift lazily over Emily before deliberately meeting her eyes. "Luckily for both of us, darlin'…that schooling is *not* going to come from me."

"WELL, IF YOU ASK ME," Simone Saunders said two hours later, "I think you should just relax about the whole thing."

"Easier said than done," Emily murmured, arranging trays of fruit cobbler and pecan-pie bars on the banquet tables set up on the town square.

"You never know," the Daybreak Café's assistant chef teased. "The guy your parents want you to meet could be a real hottie."

Emily regarded the petite dynamo with the copper colored hair. Simone was not only her trusted employee but also a close friend. "Don't you start! Besides, aren't you the one who has been extolling the virtues of freedom since your divorce?"

Simone cast a worried look at her increasingly rebellious fifteen-year-old son, Andrew, who was hanging out with a group of friends on the other side of the green. "My situation is different. My husband was a crook."

Who was now in jail, Emily thought.

"Any guy your parents want you to meet would at least be honorable."

True. Emily shrugged. "I like nice guys, but there has to be chemistry." It couldn't just be conjured up on demand.because her parents wanted it to be.

With Dylan Reeves on the other hand… Emily still couldn't believe the audacious cowboy had turned her down, and so rudely! Put his hands on her shoulders and invaded her space.

Simone glanced at the fast-growing crowd, then reached for another tray of brownies off the pastry cart. "How are you going to explain not having a date with the horse whisperer after you told your brothers you did?"

Good question. Emily added apricot scones to the table. "I could always say something came up, that Dylan wanted to attend but just couldn't."

"Uh…no…you can't."

Emily brought the buckets of fresh churned ice cream out of the portable cooler, and set them in tubs of ice on the buffet table. "Why not?"

"Because Dylan's here. Talking to Holden and Hank right now."

Heat flooding her cheeks, Emily turned around. Sure enough, Dylan Reeves *was* here, looking mighty fine in a starched white shirt, a clean pair of jeans and a black Resistol hat. It was all she could do not to wring her hands in dismay. "Holden and Hank are probably grilling him on why he didn't accompany me. If Dylan tells them I asked him for a date and he turned me down, I'll just die of embarrassment."

"Maybe he won't."

And maybe, Emily thought, already tossing her chef's apron aside, there was only one way she could stop this. She hoped it wasn't too late. "Are you okay here?"

Simone nodded, her expression as resolute as Emily's

mood. "I'll handle this. You go do damage control. And from the looks of it," Simone said softly, as the men's faces grew serious, "you better hurry."

"So what's going on with you and my sister?" Holden McCabe asked.

Didn't Emily's brothers ever lighten up? Dylan wondered, resenting the polite chitchat that was fast turning into a McCabe family inquisition.

Dylan folded his arms in front of him. "I make it a policy never to discuss my personal affairs." Not that there was anything to report.

Hank McCabe paused. He exchanged confused looks with his brother, then turned back to Dylan. "So the two of you are dating?" he asked finally.

Dylan was still contemplating how best to respond when Emily rushed up, looking gorgeous, flushed and a bit disheveled. Not that he was noticing the way the sunshine-yellow sundress hugged her slender waist and feminine curves. Or how sexy her legs looked when not encased in the usual jeans.

"Holden...Hank, for heaven's sake!" she scolded.

Predictably, her ridiculously overprotective brothers refused to back down.

"What's the problem?" Hank asked.

Holden added innocently, "We're just talking to your 'date' here."

Emily swirled around in a drift of jonquil perfume he found amazingly enticing. She shot Dylan a beseeching glance that only he could see. Her soft-as-silk hand curved possessively around his biceps, compelling him to remain silent.

Curious as to how she was going to get herself out of this mess, he merely smiled.

The panicked look in her blue eyes fading, Emily released

her grip on him and turned back to her brothers. "*Dating* is for teenagers, guys."

More skeptical glances. "What does that mean?" Holden demanded.

"It means she doesn't like to put a label on things any more than I do," Dylan intervened.

"And neither of us like answering nosy questions," Emily added.

Holden shrugged, unrepentant. "You're the one who brought it up." He turned to Dylan. "Emily told us earlier that the two of you had a date tonight."

Jeb sauntered up, a typical know-it-all grin on his face. "I've got to say, we didn't believe her then and given the fact the two of you arrived separately now…" He regarded his little sister suspiciously. "Now you wouldn't happen to be pulling one over on the whole family just because we're trying to set you up, would you?"

The only thing Dylan liked less than being put on the spot was seeing a strong, independent woman like Emily reduced to making up stories simply to get her interfering family out of her business.

"I can't believe you would even think that!" Emily sputtered.

Something about her vulnerability got to Dylan.

He'd never been prone to rescuing damsels in distress—because that could only lead to trouble. But this was different.

So he did the only thing that he knew would shut everyone up.

He wrapped his arm around Emily's slender shoulders, pivoted her slightly and brought her all the way against him.

Chapter Two

Shock rendered Emily completely still. She couldn't believe Dylan was about to kiss her, but she could not deny the electric jolt of the first brush of his lips. Suddenly breathless, she found herself closing her eyes and parting her lips. Darn it all, this reckless cowboy was one fine kisser. And she was susceptible as could be to the seductive heat of his mouth, combined with the masculine certainty of his tall, strong body pressed against hers. Despite her efforts to remain immune to this ridiculously false display of affection, she impulsively wound her arms around his neck. And still he kept on kissing her, until she shivered with sheer pleasure and the rest of the world literally fell away…

Dylan hadn't meant to get so caught up in the moment. And maybe he wouldn't have, had Emily's lips not been so incredibly sweet, her body so warm and womanly…. This was *supposed* to be his chance to put the audacious heiress in her place and make sure she never made false claims about the two of them again.

And yet, the kiss that had started out merely as a way to knock her off balance and show her who was boss swiftly turned into much, much more. It was an invitation to delve further into the chemistry between them. A lightning bolt of desire that instinct told him neither of them would soon forget.

He might not be the right kind of guy for her, or she the right kind of woman for him, but the passion between them was potent. Too potent, Dylan decided, for the kiss to continue.

It took everything he had to let the passionate embrace come to a halt. And a second after that he was reminded that they had an audience.

All three of her big brothers looked at him as if they wanted to clock him.

Dylan could hardly blame them.

Had Emily been *his* wildly impetuous baby sister…

Blushing, Emily stepped back slightly, grabbed Dylan's sleeve and held on tight. "You know," she said, seemingly making up words on the fly with the same impetuousness that had him kissing her, "that wasn't the smartest move either of us has ever made, Dylan. But," she continued before any of the four males around her could interrupt, "that's what happens when you're in love." She paused to beam at him. "Right, Dylan?"

Once again, he had a chance to put her in place. All he had to do was disavow having any feelings at all for her. Tell the truth about their "date."

Certainly, it would have been the wise thing to do—if he wanted to end this craziness.

For some reason, he didn't.

Dylan rocked back on his heels, braced his hands on his waist and shrugged in the direction of her outraged brothers. "I'm not sure there are words that would ever adequately explain this situation," he said.

"You've got that right," Emily concurred. "Besides, we should get a move on. We have to go back to the café and pick up the rest of the desserts for the buffet." She dropped her grip on his sleeve, clasped his hand in hers and tugged Dylan away from her still-scowling, perplexed brothers. "See you later, guys!" She tossed the dismissive words over her shoulder.

Seconds later, Dylan felt Emily begin to disengage her hand from his.

Loath to let her go—because that would have meant he was letting her call *all* the shots, which was not a good precedent to set—Dylan held tight.

She turned, flashed a smile that did not reach her pretty eyes and then whirled around and kept going.

Half a block of historic downtown buildings later, she had unlocked the front door to the Daybreak Café, stormed inside and shut the door behind them. Still fuming, she promptly wrested her hands from his. "All right, cowboy!" she snapped, pausing only to give him a long, withering glare. "You have one heck of a lot of explaining to do!"

EMILY EXPECTED an apology. It was, after all, the only decent thing to do, given the outlandishly passionate way Dylan had just kissed her. In front of an audience of her family and countless others, no less!

"Hey." Dylan mocked her impudently. "I'm not the one still claiming to have a date with a person who's already rejected me!"

Indignation warmed Emily's cheeks. "Claim what you like, cowboy, if it soothes your ruffled feelings, but there was nothing 'rejecting' about that kiss you just gave me."

"I never said I didn't *desire* you," Dylan volleyed back in a low, rich voice that practically oozed testosterone.

He was acting as if their madcap embrace was a *good* thing. "How dare you, anyway!"

He stepped forward and further invaded her space. "How dare you?"

With effort, Emily ignored the sexual tremors starting deep inside her. Determined to get command of a situation that was fast escalating out of control, she extended her index finger and tapped him on the center of his rock-solid chest. "Let's get something straight, Dylan." She waited until she was certain she had his full attention. "My request for help did not include anything sexual."

He winked at her facetiously. "Too bad, 'cause if it had, I might have said yes."

Emily curtailed the urge to deck him for that remark. She didn't know what he was up to now, but she did not like it one bit. "Furthermore, you are incredibly ill-mannered."

"Never claimed to be otherwise," Dylan said with a careless shrug.

Emily arched her eyebrows and ignored his pronouncement. "And you owe me an apology for that kiss."

"You owe *me* an apology for that kiss!" he countered just as emphatically, even as her knees grew weaker still.

"Really." She lifted her chin, drew a deep breath. *"Really?"*

Dylan looked at her as if he already knew what it felt like to make love to her. "You bet your hot temper you do!"

"Listen, cowboy, I did not start that!"

He moved closer, once again towering over her. "You sure continued it enthusiastically though, didn't you?"

Darned if he hadn't made her flush all over again.

Emily's spine stiffened. "Only because I didn't want to make my brothers suspicious," she retorted, hanging on to her composure by a thread.

"Yeah, well," he pointed out glibly, "you sure failed on that count."

Emily blinked. "Are you kidding? They thought our embrace was so genuinely hot they wanted to punch you out."

And whether Dylan wanted to admit it or not, their clinch *had* been genuinely hot. As well as definitely misguided, Emily thought, pushing aside the potent fantasy this discussion was evoking.

The last thing she needed to be thinking about was kissing him again, she reminded herself firmly.

And she certainly didn't need to be imagining Dylan's beautifully muscled body stretched out alongside her own.

Or fixate on the fact that everywhere she was soft, he'd be hard. Everywhere he was male, she'd be female....

He regarded her with a devil-may-care glint in his eyes. "Your siblings wanted to throttle me because they suspected it wasn't a real date and therefore felt I had no place making out with you—on the town square no less."

"They had a point about that, Dylan. You did not have a right to haul me into your arms and plant one on me."

Dylan exhaled. "You reap what you sow, sweetheart."

The warning in his tone sent a chill down her spine. "What's that supposed to mean?"

Dylan narrowed his eyes. "I'm not interested in being one of your little projects."

Despite her desire to stay cool, calm and collected, Emily's heart beat faster. "Excuse me?"

Dylan eyed her seriously. "I wasn't in town five minutes before I heard all about how the beautiful Emily McCabe likes to bring home 'strays' and fix 'em up...and then gets them to fall in love with her before she dumps them."

More like the guys dumped me, Emily thought glumly.

But not about to correct Dylan on that, she let the misconception stand.

She gave him an arch look and started to turn away. "I don't deny I was trying to help you, too." *My mistake!*

He caught her by the elbow and reeled her back. "By ensnaring me in your web so you could make me over, too?"

"You could use a few more manners, not to mention a haircut and a decent shave," she said tartly. "But that's hardly the point."

He snorted in exasperation. "Then what is?"

"Your horse-training business here in Laramie is only a couple of years older than my business." Searching for a theory he might accept as plausible, she continued making it up as she went. "I know you're constantly trying to improve the facilities and equipment on your ranch, and I thought free meals here might help your bottom line."

He glared at her. "First of all, I'm paid very well for the problem horses I diagnose and train—and I have no shortage of work coming my way. So my bottom line is fine, thank you very much."

And yet, Emily noted, she had somehow struck a nerve with her mention of money....

Her pulse inexplicably picking up, she angled her head at him. "If business is so good, why don't you hire some cowboys to help you?"

Dylan grimaced. "I like working alone. I don't want to be responsible for anyone else's livelihood. And most important of all, I don't ever want to invest so much in a piece of property that I can't pick up and move the whole operation if—and when—I feel like it."

Emily had the feeling he was talking about much more than just his ranch now. She shook her head in mocking censure. "That's a crying shame, cowboy. You'll never put down roots that way. Never belong. Probably never marry and have a family, either!"

Although why that should bother her, she did not know. It wasn't any of her business!

Dylan's broad shoulders stiffened. "I don't want roots. Or marriage. Or any of the happily-ever-afters you're peddling, because that's never been for me, either. I want my freedom. Which is why I would never—and I repeat, *never*—hook up with a down-home family gal like you."

Emily inhaled the sandalwood-and-spice fragrance of his

cologne. "I don't deny I love my family, but I am my own person."

A victorious light gleamed in his golden brown eyes. "Then how come they all feel they need to find your boyfriends for you?"

Emily bit down on a most unladylike oath. She threw up her hands in frustration, hating the fact she had to practically beg this temperamental cowpoke to cooperate. But the fix-up currently being engineered by her parents—not to mention those of her three brothers' machinations—remained a very big problem. One she was determined to solve.

Hopefully, with his help.

Emily inhaled deeply and said in the softest, most feminine voice she possessed, "Look, Dylan, all I ask is that you pretend for just a *little* while longer that you and I are an item." She added persuasively, "It shouldn't be that hard, after the way you just kissed me."

He lifted an eyebrow, said nothing.

"My offer for free meals at the café still stands." Telling herself the end justified the means, *this once,* Emily lifted a hand airily and recklessly gave herself permission to go crazy. "You can have as many breakfasts and lunches as you like… as long as you cooperate with me." There, that ought to do it. A gal couldn't get more magnanimous than that.

He hooked his thumbs through his belt loops and rocked forward on his toes. "That's very generous of you, Miss Emily."

Emily flushed at the sudden moniker of respect. "Thank you."

He lowered his handsome face until they were nose to nose. "But if I were to agree—and that in itself is a long shot—that is not the payment I want."

Oh, dear heaven.

How was it he knew just what buttons to push with her?

"Then what compensation do you want?" she asked sweetly, fearing she already knew.

"This."

Bringing his lips even closer, he cupped a hand beneath her chin. Emily could not believe he was about to kiss her again. Or worse, that she was welcoming his attentions! What kind of fool did that make her? She knew this didn't mean anything to him. Not what it should have anyway, for someone kissing her with this much passion.

Behind them, a bell rang.

Abruptly aware they were no longer alone, Emily turned her head slightly without actually stepping out of the circle of Dylan's arms. To her dismay, her parents walked in the door.

DYLAN STEPPED BACK as Shane and Greta McCabe stared at him in mute amazement. He could hardly blame them. What had gotten into him? He was usually so controlled.

Whenever he was around Emily, he acted like a hormone-driven teenager—and she was behaving just as badly. Except right now, she looked as if she wished a hole in the floor would open up so she could sink right through it.

He felt the same.

This was not the way he wanted the respected horse rancher and his accomplished wife to see him. Especially given all he now had at stake, with a soon-to-be-announced deal Emily apparently knew nothing about. Otherwise, Dylan was sure she would have mentioned it.

Not about to apologize for kissing Emily—even if it would smooth over what was an incredibly awkward situation—Dylan nodded at the older couple. He said formally, "Mr. and Mrs. McCabe. Nice to see you."

"Good to see you, Dylan," Shane and Greta McCabe replied, in unison.

"Emily." A cautioning lilt was in Greta McCabe's tone as she took in her daughter. "Your father and I just met the proprietor of the new restaurant."

"I hope he's not the guy you're planning to fix me up with," Emily said.

For some reason, Dylan noted, that notion seemed to amuse them.

"Ah—no," Shane said finally.

Unconvinced, Emily narrowed her eyes at her parents. "You're sure?"

"Absolutely," Greta said, her tone definitive.

"Because I can see how that would seem to make sense to you," Emily continued, working up a head of steam. "Me and the new diner owner, becoming a thing."

"Believe us," her mother said firmly, "the two of you are *not* a match your father and I would ever try and make."

"That's too bad," said a smug teenager with trendy, bleached-blond-hair, catching the tail end of their conversation as he sauntered in to join them.

He was just under six feet tall, wearing a burnt-orange Cowtown Diner T-shirt, jeans and the most ridiculously expensive and ornate pair of ostrich boots and gold belt buckle Dylan had ever seen.

Ignoring him, the kid grinned at Emily and extended his hand. "Because I would very much like to get to know…and date…you!"

EMILY'S JAW DROPPED even as she did the polite thing and accepted the proffered greeting.

"Xavier Shillingsworth, owner of the soon-to-be-open Cowtown Diner." The teen continued holding her hand long after it would have been polite to let go. He leaned in even closer, inundating Emily with expensive cologne. "And you must be the Emily McCabe, head chef and owner of the Day-break Café, that I've heard so much about."

Emily forced a smile and wrested her hand from the young man's grip. "Yes. I am."

Xavier continued sizing her up with undisguised interest. "I hear we're going to be in hot competition with each other—since our two restaurants are the only table-service establishments in Laramie that serve breakfast."

Emily had been brought up to be courteous, even to those who were pushy and borderline rude. And that rule went double in business situations. "I'm sure there is room for both of our establishments," she said pleasantly, injecting the situation with the down-home hospitality for which Laramie, Texas, was known.

"If not, may the best restaurateur win," Xavier taunted. Grinning confidently, he aimed a thumb at his chest and proclaimed, "I know who my money's on!"

The look in his eyes briefly telegraphing he'd had enough, Dylan stepped forward, putting his tall body between Xavier and Emily. "I don't believe we've met. I'm Dylan Reeves. One of the ranchers in the area. And I know a lot of people here tonight who would like to meet you, too. Especially Emily's three brothers. So why don't we go—" Dylan slapped a companionable hand on Xavier's shoulder and spun him around toward the door "—and talk up your new establishment."

Quick steps were made, and the door shut behind them.

"That was nice of Dylan," Greta said.

"No kidding." Emily breathed a sigh of relief.

Shane shook his head. "Shillingsworth is going to be unpleasantly competitive."

Emily rolled her eyes. "You think?"

"So, if you need help putting him in his place..." Shane growled, all protective father.

Emily lifted a palm. "I can handle the situation, Dad. Just

like I can figure out, on my own, how to rev up my personal life."

"So it's true?" her mom interrupted, with furrowed brow. "You do have a date with Dylan this evening?"

Talk about putting her on the spot! "In a manner of speaking…" Emily cleared her throat uncomfortably. "I know you mean well, but I really don't need any help finding a man to hang out with. So I'd rather not hear any suggestions on who I should be seeing. And I certainly don't want to be fixed up on any dates by anyone in the family!"

Finished, Emily braced herself for the emotional argument sure to come. Instead, to her utter amazement, her mother completely backed off. "You're right," Greta murmured, looking at Shane for verification, as if wanting to make sure they were on the same page.

Shane locked eyes with Greta. Something passed between them. "It would be a mistake for us to try to matchmake at this point," Emily's father concluded finally.

Well, that was easy, Emily thought with relief. Astoundingly…almost suspiciously…so.

"We came in to tell you that the opening ceremony is about to start," Greta said.

"I'll be right there," Emily promised. "I just need to get a few trays of chocolate and lemon-meringue pies."

"We'll all help," her dad said.

Five minutes later, the pies were set out on the buffet tables. Shane and Greta—the charity event's hosts—were stepping up to the microphones. They spoke about the Libertyville Boys Ranch, and how much the facility helped juvenile delinquents turn their lives around.

"The institution has been so successful, they are expanding again. The problem is, they need more therapy horses for the kids to care for. So," Shane said, "I've made arrangements with the Bureau of Land Management to purchase three wild mustangs for training. Dylan Reeves—the renowned horse whisperer in the area—is going to be doing the schooling." Wild applause erupted. "When they are ready, the horses will go to the boys ranch, where they will be adopted into a very good home…."

Incredibly impressed, Emily made her way through the crowd to Dylan's side. In shock, she murmured, "I had no idea you were a philanthropist."

Was it possible the two of them had more in common than they knew?

Not surprisingly, Dylan looked irritated by her compliment. "Don't view me as some sort of saint. I'm not," he muttered gruffly, and then for good measure, added, "I'm being paid."

"Just not your normal rate," Emily guessed.

Dylan scowled. "It's a challenge," he said flatly. "I like working with mustangs. I like the fact the horses will find a good, loving home at the boys ranch." He regarded her, all tough lonesome cowboy. "Don't make more of it than that."

HOURS LATER, Emily turned to Simone, as the after-event cleanup commenced. Emily followed Simone's gaze to where her son, Andrew, stood talking with that same group of boys.

"You're worried, aren't you?" The kids were from a neighboring town and looked like bad news.

Simone stacked serving platters onto a wheeled cart.

"I have a feeling he's going to ask me if he can go out past his curfew tonight."

"If it's not a good idea," Emily counseled, "you have every right to say no."

"I know that," Simone sighed. "It just seems like that's all I say these days."

The group of kids were edging toward a late-model pickup

truck with extra lights mounted across the top. They seemed to be encouraging Andrew to ditch the cleanup, forgo getting permission and just take off.

Emily touched Simone's arm. "Why don't you go on?"

Simone's posture relaxed with relief. "Thanks. I'll make it up to you."

"No problem."

Emily cast a glance at Dylan, who was busy helping a group of ranchers disassemble the bandstand. Her brothers were off with her dad, in another direction, taking down the strings of banners and colored lights.

Pleased the event had turned out so well, she finished loading up her cart and wheeled it in the direction of the café.

No sooner had she gotten inside than a light rap sounded on the door. Xavier Shillingsworth stepped in, all young bravura. "I was thinking…the two of us should go out on a date."

Emily did not like hurting anyone's feelings. Still, this was ludicrous and she had to make her would-be suitor realize it. "How old are you?" she asked gently.

"Nineteen." Xavier slicked back his hair with his free hand. "But that shouldn't matter."

She arched a brow. Was he talking down to her?

"You can't be *that* old."

"I'm twenty-eight," Emily said drily. "That's nine years older than you. It's a big difference."

Xavier shrugged. "Doesn't matter to me. I've always wanted to go out with a cougar. And you're hot!"

Was he serious? Apparently so.

Emily went back to loading dishes in the machine. "I'm curious. You are obviously a smart guy with a lot going for him. Why aren't you in college?"

Xavier seemed flattered by the attention. "I didn't want to go. So my dad bought me a franchise restaurant to run instead."

Of course. Can't solve a problem so throw money at it instead. And while you're at it, get the problem kid out of the picture, too.

Emily smiled with encouragement. "You both may want to rethink that. College can be a fun, exciting time…with lots of girls your own age who are dying to go out on dates."

"I don't want a girl. I want you!"

Emily sighed and walked toward the exit. "Well, it's not going to happen."

"See?" Xavier caught up with her as she reached the dining room. He clamped his arms around her and crowded her all the more. "That's what I like about you. You're a real spitfire."

Not about to let him so much as try to kiss her, Emily stomped on his toe with all her might. "And you're a real horse's rear end," she spat out.

"Ouch!" Xavier hopped up and down in pain.

The door to the café opened and Dylan strode in. It took him all of two seconds to size up the situation. "Allow me." He grabbed Xavier by the back of his Cowtown Diner T-shirt and escorted him to the door.

Dylan let him go just inside the portal. "If you ever touch her again, you're going to have to deal with me."

"On what grounds?" Xavier straightened his shirt. He regarded Dylan pugnaciously, clearly spoiling for a fistfight.

She was afraid there just might be one if the kid didn't cut it out.

"I don't see an engagement ring!"

Eager to be rid of the callow youth, Emily swung open the door to the café and glared at the teenager. "I don't need a ring to be his. Now go."

"You heard the lady." When Xavier didn't immediately comply, Dylan shoved him out the door and shut it firmly in his face.

Emily turned to Dylan. She knew it was unnecessary and

politically incorrect of her, but she really liked the idea of Dylan jumping to her defense. Unfortunately, it wasn't an action she could let stand as precedent.

She rolled her eyes comically. "Obviously, I was exaggerating...about being your woman."

The way Dylan was looking at her—as if he didn't know whether to kiss her or chide her—forced Emily to remember exactly how good it had felt to be held in his embrace.

"I am aware of that," he retorted.

"And for the record," Emily continued stiffly, telling herself she and Dylan would not end up kissing again, no matter what, "I don't need you to come to my rescue."

The corners of Dylan's lips twitched. "It would appear you did."

Was it possible he had enjoyed defending her honor as much as she had? Emily pushed the bothersome thought away.

"No," she corrected forcing herself to stay on track. She needed to keep her emotions under wraps. "I didn't."

"Uh-huh." Dylan came closer, all sexy, determined male. "If you change your mind..."

Emily's pulse jumped. "Why would I do that?"

"Because guys like that don't like to be told no," Dylan said in a low, cautioning tone.

Emily had been successfully fighting her own battles for as long as she could recall. "Well, in this case the kid is going to have to get used to it, because I am not interested in being his cougar."

One corner of Dylan's mouth curved upward at the notion. "He actually said that?"

So, she wasn't the only one who found the teen's proposal to her completely ludicrous!

"It was part of his come-on," she explained. "I think in Xavier's teenage fantasy I was just supposed to melt in his arms or something."

Dylan grunted in response, his disapproval evident.

"Anyway," Emily rushed on, anxious to put the embarrassing situation behind her, "I'm sure that after what just happened he'll leave me alone now."

Dylan's expression was suddenly as inscrutable as his posture. Deliberately, he inclined his head. "If he doesn't…you're welcome to be 'my woman'…anytime."

Chapter Three

"Dylan Reeves really called you *his woman?*" Simone echoed in the café kitchen early the following day.

Doing her best to keep her focus on getting ready for the morning rush, Emily shrugged nonchalantly. "He was mocking me because of what I said to that boy in the heat of the moment." The fact that Emily warmed from head to toe, every time she recalled it, was her own foolishness. "Obviously, Dylan didn't mean it because it's not true." She brought an extra large pan of golden-brown cinnamon rolls from the oven, and slid in a pan of buttermilk biscuits.

Simone manned the sausage and bacon on the griddle. She winked. "He could be—if you wanted it. Seriously…he's got the hots for you."

Emily guffawed. "You only wish my life were that exciting. Dylan is the kind of guy who roots for the underdog in every situation and he thought I was disadvantaged in that moment."

"Were you?"

Emily gave the hash-brown potatoes a stir. "I had just stomped on Xavier's toes and planned to escort him to the door. But…Dylan beat me to it."

"Wow…" Simone comically fanned her chest. "Two men fighting over you."

Emily blushed despite herself. "I wouldn't call Xavier a man," she said.

"I know." Sympathetic, Simone furrowed her brow. "What's up with that? How old is he?"

"Nineteen."

"That is way too young to be running a restaurant," Simone said.

"No kidding. But I imagine he's going to find that out the hard way."

The bell on the service door sounded, as Billy Ray and Bobbie Sue Everett came in. The married couple waited tables at the café during the day and attended community-college classes at night. Normally very down-to-earth and unflappable, they were giddy with excitement. "You-all have got to see this. We've never seen anything like this!"

All four of them rushed to the front windows. Dawn was barely streaking across the sky, but there it was—on the opposite side of the Laramie town square—a big burnished-bronze trailer-style restaurant, with an old-style saloon front, sitting on top of an enormous tractor-trailer bed. Next to it was the enormous crane that would move the Cowtown Diner onto the lot where a gas station had once stood.

Emily's heart sank. It really was happening.

"Can you believe it's actually going to be open for business by the end of the week?" Billy Ray said.

Aware the customers would soon be lining up outside the door to be let in when the café opened at six o'clock, Emily went back to the kitchen and brought out the platters of homemade cinnamon rolls and sticky buns that would be on display.

"It's only possible," Emily said, "because the building is delivered ready to go and everything they serve in the restaurant is prepackaged and pre-made."

"It's still amazing," Bobbie Sue murmured, while quickly helping her husband set up the tables.

Emily had a sinking feeling her customers were going to think so, too.

THE LUNCH CROWDS WERE finally thinning when Dylan walked into the café at one-thirty, so he was able to get a table right away. To his surprise, Emily came out of the kitchen personally to bring him a menu. After the events of the previous day, he had suspected she might try to avoid him. He couldn't blame her; he had done as much this very morning, choosing to eat breakfast on the ranch instead of coming to the café, as usual.

But then he'd thought about it and decided that was pure foolishness. He was blowing this all out of proportion and really wanted to get back on solid ground with her.

"I don't need to see that," Dylan said, determined to keep the exchange as casual as possible. "I memorized the offerings on your menu the first week you opened."

And like most ranchers in the area, he had been eating her "cowboy cuisine" frequently ever since.

"You sure? I've put a few new things on the menu, just today."

He was sure. But since it seemed to mean so much to her, he opened the laminated menu anyway. A hand-lettered inset offered two new sandwiches and a fried jalapeño-cheese popper appetizer that was a customer favorite at the Cowtown Diner chain. "Competing already?" he drawled.

He'd figured the sight of the rival establishment would have upped Emily's competitive spirit.

Curious to know just how far she would go, he leaned back in the red vinyl booth and prodded, "Or just stealing another restaurant's signature dish?"

She ran her hand lightly over the red-and-white-checked oilcloth. "Ha-ha."

"You're better than that. Your food is better than that."

Her feisty gaze met his once again. "Says the man with the bottomless pit for a stomach."

Well, at least she still had her temper. Enjoying the exchange more than he had a right to, he angled a thumb at his chest. "Hey—you make a lot of money off me."

Emily folded her arms in front of her. "Not today, since I assume you are here to collect on my promise of free food for however long you want it."

Was it possible that the feisty, inimitable Emily McCabe was actually depressed? Dylan didn't want to think so, but there was something different about her eyes.

"I'll have the chicken-fried steak meal with all the vegetables you got, biscuits, a strong pot of coffee and two glasses of water, to start. We'll see about dessert later."

Their fingers brushed briefly as Emily took the menu and insert back. Dylan wondered if she'd thought about their kisses as much as he had last night and today. Not that it mattered, he told himself, since it wasn't going to happen again.

"And be sure you bill me for every last morsel," he added sternly.

Emily arched a delicate eyebrow.

He looked her square in the eye. "No lady pays my way."

Emily laughed out loud, ready to challenge him on that and a few other things. "So now you're calling me a lady?" Her bow-shaped lips curling in an appreciative smirk, she pocketed the order pad in her apron.

That was a lot less dangerous than calling her "his woman." Dylan figured they both had to know that.

He worked to get their conversation back on its usual smart-aleck track. "And a hothead. Not to mention a damn fine cook."

Abruptly, moisture gleamed in Emily's eyes.

Before he could question her about it, she ducked her head and turned to leave. "Coming right up," she said hoarsely over her shoulder.

Five minutes later, Bobby Sue was there with his dinner. It was as hot and fresh and delicious as always.

Dylan downed it all with relish.

He was considering whether or not he had time to order dessert before the café closed at two, when Emily's father walked in.

Dessert was going to have to wait, because he had business to conduct.

Dylan stood to greet the elder McCabe, as previously arranged. "Everything going okay so far?" he asked.

Shane nodded. "The horse trailers are due to arrive any minute."

Emily walked out of the kitchen. Obviously surprised to see Dylan standing there with her dad, she looked from one to the other. "What's going on?"

Shane greeted his daughter with a hug.

"The mustangs are coming in. We decided to meet up here because I thought you might like to take a peek at them before they're taken to Dylan's ranch."

That swiftly, the light was back in Emily's eyes. She smiled, her love of horses as apparent as ever. "I would. Thanks, Dad." She hugged her father, then turned to Dylan awkwardly. She started forward, as if to hug him, too, then reconsidered and made do with a shy nod. "Dylan. This was nice of you."

He cleared his throat. "No problem."

Emily turned back to her dad. "Tell me about the horses," she said eagerly.

"Two of them are less than twelve months old. They're traveling two to a trailer, as per bureau of land management rules. The three-year-old mare is in a stock trailer by herself.

She's not yet fence- or halter-broken and may be a problem when it comes to unloading her."

Dylan figured that was an understatement. "Any of them got names?" he asked Shane.

The older gentleman shook his head. "Just registration numbers. So feel free to name them whatever you see fit while you're training them."

Simone's son, Andrew, walked in on the tail end of the conversation. A backpack slung over his shoulder, he appeared ready to assume his duties as part-time dishwasher and kitchen help. He looked at his mom, who'd come out of the restaurant kitchen. "Can I go see the horses? Maybe help the guys unload them?"

Simone shook her head. "It's too dangerous, honey."

Andrew's expression fell. "But…"

"And you have homework to do, don't you?" Simone insisted.

"Well, yeah," the fifteen-year-old admitted with a reluctant shrug, "but…"

"You'll have a chance to see the mustangs later," Simone promised. "When they're tamed."

Andrew sulked. "That'll be forever."

"Knowing Dylan and the magic he works, probably not as long as you think." Simone put her hand on her son's shoulder. "Right now you and I need to help Bobbie Sue and Billy Ray get the kitchen closed for the day. See you later, everyone." The two of them went back into the café kitchen.

Emily glanced out the window at the commotion outside. "Looks like they're here," she said, and smiled.

Shane turned back to Emily. "Do you have plans for this evening? Because if you don't, your mother and I would like you to come over to the dance hall and have dinner with us. Maybe do a little brainstorming about how you're going to weather this new competition?"

Emily bucked at the fatherly interference, even as she started for the door. "Thanks, Dad," she said over one slender shoulder, "but I've got it covered."

Shane persisted. "Just dinner, then?"

Emily pressed her lips together firmly. "I can't." Her glance shifted to Dylan's face. She gave him the look that beseeched him to play along with her. "I'm going out to Dylan's ranch, to help him get the mustangs settled."

Dylan felt for Emily. It couldn't be fun to be on the end of such constant meddling. But that didn't mean he wanted to sacrifice his own professional standing with her father—one of the most respected horse-ranchers in the state—just so she did not have to do her parents' bidding.

He tamped down his own irritation. "That's okay, Emily," Dylan said just as firmly, holding her glance deliberately. "I think I've got it."

"Oh, I know you *could* do it without me." Emily slipped out onto the street and strode toward the horse trailers, as excited and energetic as the animals whinnying in the confines. "But I really don't want to miss this!"

"AT WHAT POINT are you going to stop using me to dodge your familial difficulties?" Dylan asked Emily, after the papers transferring financial responsibility to Shane and care of the mustangs to Dylan were signed and they were headed out to their vehicles.

"Never?" Emily paused at the door of her car.

Dylan peered down at her. "Think again."

She hit the unlock button on the automatic keypad. "Look, I owe you for last night, and thus far you've refused to let me pay you back with free food, so I'm left to come up with another way to pay off my debt. This is it."

Dylan curved a hand over the top of her open door as she

climbed in behind the wheel. He leaned down so they were face to face. "I repeat. You do not have to do this."

"Sure I do. For the very same reason you don't ever let a lady pay your way."

He should have known she would use his words against him.

She smiled, unperturbed. "So I'll help you with the mustangs."

Damn, if she wasn't used to getting her own way, even if it meant upsetting the hard-earned tranquility of his life.

"Just understand," Dylan said, "when you're out there, playtime is over. I'm putting you to work."

Turning the key in the ignition, she shot him a sassy look. "Bring it on!"

EMILY COULDN'T WAIT to get a good look at the horses. She bounded out of her car the moment she arrived at Dylan's ranch. She set her hat on her head and strode toward him. "What do you want me to do?"

Dylan turned, all business and all cowboy. "Honestly? Stay out of the way," he said, grimacing.

Emily blew out a disappointed breath. Before she could figure out how to persuade him otherwise, he took a step closer and growled, "I mean it, Emily. I don't want you getting trampled."

Emily followed him over to a big round corral with high metal-bar sides. "I've been around horses all my life."

Dylan opened the gate wide and motioned for the truck carrying the two yearlings. He directed the driver to back slowly toward the opening. "These mustangs are completely different from the domesticated cutting horses your father breeds and trains. These horses are wild, down to the core."

Hand to her shoulder, Dylan guided her to the outside of

the pen, then walked back around to the rear of the enclosed vehicle.

Emily's heartbeat picked up as he opened the trailer and let the first horse out.

It was a filly, about six months old, with a speckled white coat and an ivory mane, her beauty marred only by the identifying freeze marks on her neck. She whinnied as she came barreling out of confinement and raced to the other end of the pen. Emily could see she was frightened—she was standing with her tail puckered tight against her hindquarters and the back of her legs.

Dylan stood quietly, as did Emily, as the filly trembled and kept her head up.

Dylan let the second horse out—a jet-black gelding about a year old. His head was up, too—his tail wringing in anger. Obviously, he had not appreciated the long ride. Or maybe the procedure that had put the freeze marks on his neck, Emily thought. He galloped across the pen, his ebony mane flying, and took a protective position next to the smaller white filly.

They were already forming a herd, Emily thought.

Moving purposefully and calmly, Dylan stepped out and shut the gate. The first truck drove off.

The next trailer backed toward the pen.

When it was in position, Dylan opened the gate and released the third horse.

Emily caught her breath as the mare kicked and bucked her way out of the trailer. The color of ginger, she had darker-colored legs, a dark ginger mane and a striking white blaze down her forehead. Her tail was stiff and pointed up as she kicked and reared her way across the pen. Once near the other horses, she raised up on her hind legs again, her ears pinned back, whinnying furiously at the humans she blamed for her captivity.

Turning her rear to the other two horses, she backed up and pawed the ground.

Dylan smiled.

So did Emily.

"No doubt who is in charge of the herd," she said, nodding at the ginger mare.

The question was, who was going to be in charge of her and Dylan—if she spent any time alone with him? She'd only been around him a short while and she was already thinking about how thrilling it would be to kiss him again.

"So what next?" Willfully, Emily turned her attention back to the mustangs.

"I let them settle in for a few days to recover from the trip, get used to their surroundings and begin to trust this is a place they are going to like."

Made sense. "When it's time, I'd like to help you with their training," Emily offered.

Dylan glanced at her skeptically. For reasons she did not understand, his doubt hurt. "Don't think I can do it?"

Dylan shook his head and sauntered toward the barn. "Let's just say I don't think your family would approve."

Emily followed. "It wouldn't be the first time."

For some reason, Emily thought, that struck a chord—one he didn't like.

He let his glance trail over her, lazily inspecting every curve, before returning to her face. "You have a major challenge facing your business." He picked up a bale of hay and carried it back over to the corral. "Why don't you concentrate on that?"

Emily watched him cut the twine, holding it together. She scoffed and folded her arms across her chest. "I can do both."

"Really?" Methodically, Dylan broke up the square of crisp

sweet hay. He tossed it over the fence. "Then you must be a superwoman."

Emily watched the mustangs. The herd was still on the other side of the pen but contemplating every move Dylan made. "I am an excellent horsewoman."

Dylan threw out the last of the feed and exhaled in frustration. He slowly straightened and poked up the brim of his hat. "Why don't you do us both a favor, Emily, and stick to cooking?"

Emily didn't know whether to slug him or kiss him. Truth was, she wanted to do both. "Why won't you let me help?"

Her pique increased his own irritation. "Because you don't work for me." He walked over to turn on the spigot and fill the trough with water. "I don't have enough liability insurance. I don't have time to train them and you, too. Pick a reason."

The mustangs made their way stealthily toward the feed. "Can I at least come by and watch from time to time?"

He rubbed the underside of his jaw, testing the stubble of afternoon beard. Their glances met and held. "If I say no, will you stay away?"

Emily offered a careless shrug. "Maybe." The silence between them drew out, prompting her to eventually admit, with a reluctantly candid sigh, "Maybe not."

His expression hardened. "That's what I thought."

She didn't know why she wanted his respect so badly in this regard, she just knew that she did, and she wished he would give her a chance to earn it. "Dylan—"

He turned off the spigot with a harsh twist.

His eyes narrowed as he regarded her intently. "Do us both a favor, Emily. Go back to your family. Work out whatever needs to be worked out." He lifted a gloved hand before she could interrupt. "And leave me—and these horses—out of it."

LATE THE FOLLOWING AFTERNOON, Dylan answered another summons from Shane McCabe. He met with Emily's father in the study of the Circle M Ranch house, where they discussed the condition of the mustangs and Dylan's plan for training them.

It was a cordial, productive meeting and, despite himself, Dylan found himself warming to the elder rancher.

Usually, he did not care for men of such power and wealth, although he never minded doing business with them. Money was money, and they easily paid the fees Dylan commanded.

At the conclusion of their discussion, Shane handed Dylan a check, as previously agreed upon. "This should cover your time and the expenses of caring for the mustangs for the first month. If you need anything else, be sure and let me know."

"Thank you."

Before Dylan could get up, Shane said, "If you've got a moment, I'd like to speak with you about the Libertyville Boys Ranch. The director—Mike Harrigan—is a friend of mine. He mentioned your devotion to the facility."

This was headed toward territory Dylan had no wish to discuss. He lifted a hand to cut off the discussion. "It's no big deal."

Shane leaned forward earnestly. "On the contrary, it's a very big deal, Dylan. The boys ranch turns a lot of young lives around. I want to do more than just provide a few horses. So here's what I was thinking…" Shane elaborated for the next few minutes. Finally, he finished, "And given your expertise in this area, I'd really like your help in making that dream a reality."

The offer was unexpected. And amazing. Not to mention out of the question. "Thank you, sir. I'll do what I can to contribute to your efforts."

"But?" Shane sensed a catch.

"I don't think I am the right man for the setup you have in mind. I'll continue training the mustangs and then hand them over to the Libertyville Boys Ranch as promised. But that's really all I can guarantee, in terms of helping you out."

Shane had the same look on his face that Emily had on hers whenever Dylan told her no. The one that said a McCabe wasn't giving up on what they wanted, no matter what obstacles lay in front of them.

Finally, Shane rocked back in his chair.

Dylan expected Emily's father to say something like the offer was always going to be open. Instead, he steepled his hands in front of him and inquired, "So what's going on with you and my daughter?"

Dylan swore silently to himself. For the life of him he did not know how to answer that. There was desire, certainly. And he really liked her cooking. But beyond that...

His concern for his only daughter apparent, Shane continued, "I've never seen her run after anyone the way she's been chasing you." He paused. "Usually, it's the other way around. Guys are beating down her door."

Dylan had been around long enough to know that to be true. Not that Emily had been inclined, in the past year or so anyway, to let anyone make much of a move on her. As far as he knew, she hadn't even had a date—not counting the pretend one with him.

"So..." Shane stood and looked at Dylan, man-to-man. "If I may...a word of advice?"

Dylan took the cue and got to his feet, too. He honored the elder horseman with a look of respect.

"If you don't think you will ever be serious about Emily... then do whatever you have to do..." Shane said, firmly, "but don't let my daughter catch you."

DYLAN WALKED OUT the front door of the Circle M Ranch house, still contemplating the counsel from Shane McCabe.

As much as he hated having others meddle in his business, Emily's father was right.

Emily might think she was a free spirit, but she was also vulnerable and traditional to the core.

A wild affair would never make her happy. Nor would deceiving her loved ones.

Not in the long term.

And for some reason he couldn't figure, Dylan wanted to see the pretty brunette happy.

Which made what came next all the more unpalatable.

Striding toward Dylan, his arms full of Cowtown Diner goodies, was Xavier Shillingsworth. The teen flashed a pretentious smile his way. "Going the wrong way there, aren't you, fella?"

There was no denying the snide undertone in his words. Or the resentment in Xavier's gaze. Dylan paused on the wide front steps of the rustic fieldstone and cedar ranch house. He did not bother to smile back. "Excuse me?"

"Hired help comes and goes from the back, right?" Xavier sneered. "So…you should have gone in and out the *back* entrance."

Dylan had suffered the taunts of the snotty rich from boyhood on. He knew he should let it go, straighten the brim of his hat, ignore the little twerp and keep moving. Yet something about the guy, and the situation, had him returning equally, "Ranchers go in the front."

"And here I thought you were just another cowboy," Xavier said, as Emily and her mother drove up in their respective vehicles.

Looking gorgeous and ready for a night out on the town, Emily was first to emerge.

Xavier shifted the stack of Cowtown Diner memorabilia

in his arms and turned to face Emily. "Going to be joining us for dinner this evening?"

"Uh, no," Emily murmured, appearing not the least bit disappointed about that.

Bypassing the teen completely, Emily walked up to Dylan and looked him straight in the eye. "May I have a word with you?"

Figuring he'd find out sooner than later why the feisty heiress was so piqued, Dylan shrugged. "Sure." He ambled down the steps alongside Emily, as Greta McCabe emerged from her Mercedes.

"Nice to see you, Dylan," Greta said pleasantly.

He briefly removed his hat in a gesture of respect. "Nice to see you, Mrs. McCabe."

"Perhaps you'd like to join us for dinner this evening, Dylan?" Greta continued pleasantly. "Emily? You, too?"

Emily perked up.

Xavier looked totally ticked off.

Which in Dylan's view, made it all worth it. "Don't mind if I do," he told Greta. It wouldn't be the first time he had dined with the Laramie, Texas, elite, but it would definitely be the most satisfying.

Chapter Four

"Mind telling me what's going on around here?" Emily asked, the moment her mother and Xavier Shillingsworth had disappeared inside the house, and shut the door behind them.

Dylan was getting a little tired of being a bit player in the McCabe family drama. He lounged against the rail edging the porch steps and folded his arms in front of him. "You're going to have to be more specific if you want me to answer that."

Emily wrapped her hand around his biceps and led him down the steps, across the yard, into the shade. "Fine. You want to cut to the chase, we'll cut right to the chase." She glared at him. "I heard you had a meeting with my father."

Man, she had a temper! Dylan couldn't help but grin. "Spies everywhere, hmm?" he teased.

Emily regarded him with greatly exaggerated patience. "My mother mentioned it in passing."

Dylan clapped a hand over his heart, mimicking her damsel-on-high-alert attitude. "Then it was top secret!"

"I'm serious." Emily stomped closer, the delicate daffodil scent of her freshly washed hair and skin teasing his senses. She'd changed out of her casual work clothes and slipped into a sexy lavender dress that clung nicely to her curves.

His eyes drifted to her feet. Instead of the usual boots,

she had on a pair of open-toed sandals, perfect for the warm spring weather.

"What did he say to you?"

Lifting his gaze, Dylan resisted the urge to touch the silky dark strands spilling loosely over her slender shoulders. Instead, he concentrated on the determined pout of her soft, sensual lips before returning his attention to her eyes. "And this is your business because…?"

She tilted her head in a discerning manner. "I know it was about me."

"Or…" He sidestepped the direct inquiry by producing the check from his shirt pocket. He waved it in front of her, like a matador taunting a bull. "Perhaps it was about…this?"

Emily exhaled loudly. "I know that's what it was about officially, dummy." Her pretty chin jutted out. "I also know he would not have missed an opportunity to privately tell you what he tells all the men I'm interested in."

Dylan liked being lumped in with her other discarded suitors about as much as he liked being interrogated. He blinked in feigned surprise. "*You're* interested in me?"

A flash of amusement sparkled in her eyes, then disappeared as quickly as it had appeared. "Ostensibly," Emily admitted. "Not really."

Dylan told himself that was irritation—not disappointment—he was feeling.

Emily paused and appeared to do a double take. "Are *you* interested in *me?*"

It was his turn to regard her with a droll expression. "What do you think?" he asked in a smart-alecky tone.

Her delicate dark eyebrows lifted. "That you are without a doubt the most infuriating man I have ever met."

Dylan noted she had enunciated every word with perfect clarity. He lifted his hat in salute and resettled it on his head. "Thank you."

Emily harrumphed. "It's nothing to be proud of."

"Maybe not in your opinion," Dylan murmured, aware he was enjoying matching wits and wills with her more than he had enjoyed anything in a long time.

Emily shook her head as if that would get her back on track. "So, why are you suddenly so eager to have dinner with me and my family?"

Good question. It couldn't be because he had started to feel protective of Emily, could it? He knew better than that. Rich heiresses were not allowed to fall for guys like him. And even if they bucked all propriety and followed their hearts, the misguided affair had little hope of lasting, because of family influence. In their case, they'd have to contend with Shane McCabe and all three of her overbearing brothers.

Aware she was still waiting for an explanation, Dylan said casually, "Maybe I'm in need of a good evening meal?"

"And maybe you're trying to get under my skin?"

"Always an unexpected bonus."

Silence fell between them.

Emily continued to study him beneath the fringe of dark lashes. "So you're not going to tell me what my dad said to you in private?" she said eventually.

And give her even more reason to rebel against her family? For both their sakes, Dylan checked his own desire. "No." He offered her his arm. "Now, shall we go in?"

DINNER WITH Emily's parents turned out to be a lot less formal, and more comfortable, than Dylan had expected.

Xavier Shillingsworth, on the other hand, was as much of a pain in the rear as ever.

The hopelessly inexperienced restaurateur commandeered the conversation from the moment the five of them sat down at the wicker-and-glass patio table, zeroing in on everything he felt was wrong with the way Emily was running the Daybreak Café.

"I don't understand why you're only open for breakfast and lunch, six days a week," Xavier told Emily. "I've seen the line of people waiting to get in. Why not serve dinner, too?"

"There are already plenty of places that serve dinner," Emily explained. "My mother's dance hall for one."

Xavier leaned across the table toward Emily. "So?"

She shrugged. "I don't want to compete with her."

Xavier frowned. "You compete with her at lunch."

Emily paused, a forkful of baby-lettuce salad halfway to her mouth. "It's not the same."

"Why not?" Xavier persisted, failing to notice the discreet looks Shane and Greta were giving each other from opposite ends of the dinner table.

Emily shifted in her chair, her knee nudging Dylan's briefly under the table. "Because the dance hall has live bands on Friday and Saturday evenings, and DJs in the evening the rest of the time."

Xavier grimaced. "So play music in your café."

"There's no room to dance," Emily said, still trying to talk sense to him.

Xavier finished his salad and pushed his plate to the side. "A lot of people don't dance anyway."

Dylan wondered if the kid thought he was going to attract Emily by criticizing her business sense. One thing was certain—he certainly wasn't scoring any points with her or her folks. And if he treated the rest of the town this way...

"The point is, there is no demand for another dinner place right now," Emily said matter-of-factly. "Laramie already has a handful of local establishments that have pretty much got the evening food covered."

"And maybe if you tried, you'd have standing-room-only

business at dinner, too, and force someone else to close down."

Eyebrows raised all around at that.

Not good, dude, Dylan thought. Not good at all...

"I think the point my daughter is trying to make," Shane McCabe cut in with remarkable kindness, "is that in Laramie, it's not just the ranchers who help each other out. The business owners look out for one another, too."

As Dylan expected, that notion didn't go down well with their teenage guest.

Greta collected the empty salad plates and replaced them with servings of Southwestern-style meat loaf, mashed potatoes and peas. "We want all the restaurants to be successful, and of course that would include yours," she told Xavier graciously.

Xavier sat up straighter, looking affronted. "I hope you're not asking me to cut back on the hours the Cowtown Diner is open."

Shane McCabe lifted a hand. "No one's going to tell you what to do. It's your business to run, after all. We're just suggesting that you might want to join the chamber of commerce and any of the other service organizations in town that interest you. It's a good way to get to know everyone and become a real part of the community."

Xavier rejected the notion with a shake of his head. "I'm not interested in charity work. The only thing on *my* mind is turning as much of a profit as soon as possible."

The kid just wasn't getting it, Dylan thought. The McCabes were offering him a hand up. And he was too clueless and arrogant to take it.

"When is the grand opening?" Dylan asked, attempting to draw some fire himself.

Xavier dismissed Dylan with a glance that revealed Xavier still considered him "hired help." "Friday."

Emily studied the teen, suddenly on edge again. "You're really going to be up and running three days from now?"

Nodding proudly, Xavier grinned at Emily. "I'll bet you can't wait."

"CAN YOU WAIT?" Dylan asked Emily an hour later, after they had thanked her parents for dinner and said their goodbyes.

"Very funny, cowboy."

Relieved that Xavier had finally rushed off to continue work on his restaurant, Emily ambled down the front steps to her car. Dylan was right beside her, a surprisingly steady presence.

"But as long as we're recapping…" Emily paused to search through her bag for her keys. She looked at Dylan, wondering what his take on the situation was. His attitude throughout the meal had been so maddeningly inscrutable that she had no clue. "What was Xavier's deal? He really went overboard with that intense interrogation."

Dylan leaned against the side of her car, one foot crossed over the other, arms folded in front of him. Dusk had given way to night, and the sky overhead was filled with a full moon and a sprinkling of stars.

He gave her a bemused look. "I think that was Xavier taking self-absorbed to new heights."

"Not to mention immaturity." Emily fished the keys out. "Can you believe his father bought him a restaurant?" She closed the clasp on her handbag. "Never mind plunked it down in Laramie, Texas, of all places?"

He moved closer, smelling like soap and man. "I'm sure they both figured there would be less competition here, and hence, it would be easier for a greenhorn like Xavier to succeed."

Emily bit her lip. Unable to take her eyes off his broad shoulders and nicely muscled chest, she said, "I suppose you're right about that. If the kid were in Dallas or Houston, it would be a much tougher road for him to travel."

"Although small towns come with challenges, too." Dylan looked over at her, seemingly in no hurry to move on. "It was nice of your parents to invite him over, though."

That was the way her folks were—generous and welcoming, to the bone. "They're just trying to bring Xavier into the 'fold' of Laramie business people. Obviously, my mother did not anticipate the way he was going to go after me with the third degree, hinting that I didn't know what I was doing, running my business." Emily sighed, still feeling a little embarrassed about that.

Dylan met her eyes. "And yet you were incredibly nice and patient with the kid, too," he observed kindly.

It hadn't been easy, given how obnoxious Xavier had been. But Emily had nevertheless tried to give the clueless teenager the benefit of the doubt. "I figure he probably doesn't know any other way to interact with people, given how he was likely raised."

Dylan lifted a brow and guessed. "With too much money and too little guidance?"

Emily nodded, aware she and Dylan were now close enough to feel each other's body heat. She swallowed and stepped back slightly. "Think about it. Rather than help Xavier deal with whatever issues he has that are keeping him from wanting to go to college with his peers, his father bought him a franchise and sent him off to the boondocks alone to run it." She frowned. "That doesn't exactly foretell a lot of tender loving care."

DYLAN KNEW what it was like to be on the receiving end of a family with too much money and too little heart. A family that just wanted you out of the way... To his surprise, he suddenly felt a little sorry for the kid. "You're right," he said quietly. "I hadn't thought about it that way."

Empathy radiated in Emily's blue eyes. "Unfortunately, Xavier won't survive in this town for long if he continues the way he has been."

"Also true," Dylan said. Kindness and concern for one's neighbor was the norm in Laramie County, not cutthroat aggression.

Emily shrugged. "So...I figured...since my parents had taken the initiative and tried to help him acclimate more successfully, I would be as compassionate as possible, too."

That would have been fine had it not been for her personal history. Dylan lifted a brow. "Another of your makeover projects?"

Just that quickly the flash of temper appeared on her face. Emily propped her hands on her hips. "That would imply Xavier and I are romantically involved," she retorted, resentment simmering in her low tone. "You know very well we're not, and are never going to be."

Dylan smiled—she had just given him the answer he was looking for. "So you admit you try and make over the guys you date?" he pressed.

Did her father also get in the act—behind the scenes, of course? Was that what had really prompted Shane's offer to him earlier?

Dylan hated to think so. He wanted to think the proposal put to him was merit-based. On the other hand, he also knew Shane and Greta McCabe adored their only daughter and would do whatever they had to do to see she was well matched.

Even by giving her current "love interest" a hand up...?

Oblivious to the downward spiral to his thoughts, Emily continued, "Isn't that what love is supposed to be about?

Changing for the better because you're involved with your ideal mate?"

Her lips looked so soft and inviting, he wondered what it would feel like to silence her with a kiss. But he told himself to stay focused. "I thought relationships were supposed to be about *not* having to change. Being adored for who and what you *already* were. What's that saying?" He attempted to lighten the mood. "'I love you just the way you are.'"

Emily scoffed. "It's a song lyric, not a saying. And for the record—" she softened her tone wistfully "—I kind of like that you-complete-me thing."

He should have figured she would be a *Jerry Maguire* fan. Knowing this had to be said if they were going to be friends, he pointed out sagely, "If the man and the woman 'complete' each other, then that would imply they can't live without the other person."

"So?"

Lazily, Dylan tracked the way the breeze was ruffling her hair. He reached over to tuck an errant strand behind her ear, then let his hand drop. "What kind of life would that be?" he asked unhappily. "If everything hinged on a person who might or might not live up to your expectations?"

IT WOULD NOT be the kind of life Dylan apparently wanted, Emily thought.

She sighed, her emotions abruptly as turbulent as his.

"Anyway," Dylan continued, dropping his hand back to his side. He studied her expression. "I'm guessing your parents don't know that Xavier hit on you."

Thrilling from his brief, casual touch, Emily turned so her back was to the car. She lounged against the driver door, wishing Dylan wasn't such a hard man to get to know. But he was extremely independent—and as emotionally elusive as the wild mustangs he was going to tame....

So she needed to forget about making him her next "diamond in the rough."

After all, there was no point in pretending he would be willing to transform himself into what she wanted—any more than she would be willing to convert into what he wanted.

"I've been trying to forget that incident with Xavier." Emily forced herself to get their conversation back on track. "And for the record, Dylan," she warned, locking gazes with him, "I would prefer my family never know about all that cougar silliness."

Suddenly, the humor was back in the situation. "Why not?" he said as his lips formed a most devil-may-care smile.

Emily's exasperation returned anew. "Because Xavier's pass was ludicrous enough without adding another layer of ridiculousness to it by having my father call him to his study and sit him down for The Talk."

Abruptly, Dylan went very still, a fact which only confirmed Emily's worst suspicions. Seeing her chance to do a little more sleuthing, she added cheekily, "You know, kind of like the one I suspect my father had with *you* today, about me?"

The kind that generally sent weaker men running for the hills...

Just like that, a wall went up. "It's not going to work, Emily." Dylan was the picture of lazy male self-assurance.

She stared at him.

He stared right back. "I'm still not telling you what was said."

Emily sighed—she could have predicted that. Pushing away from the car, she suddenly felt reinvigorated. "Then how about doing something to cheer me up instead?"

Dylan pushed away from her car, too. "And what would that be?" he inquired with mock seriousness.

"Allow me to come and visit the mustangs again," Emily said, this time stepping forward to invade his space.

Dylan stayed where he was even as respect glimmered in his eyes. "Are you going to have time?"

Emily ignored the tingle of excitement that started within her whenever they were within kissing distance. "I will if we go tonight."

For a minute, Emily thought Dylan was going to turn her down. "Isn't it a little past your bedtime?" he teased in a tone sexy enough to make her want to melt right then and there.

Stubbornly, Emily held her ground, knowing she wasn't ready for her time with Dylan to end. "It's only nine-thirty."

He continued to look down at her, considering. "And you have to go to work at four tomorrow morning."

"I can get by on very little sleep, when I want," Emily murmured in her most cajoling voice. "Please, Dylan. I've been thinking about the mustangs all day. Wondering how they're adjusting. If you've given them names yet."

Seeming to realize her interest and concern were genuine, his expression softened. "They're settling in. And no, I haven't given them names."

"Maybe I could help with that."

"Thirty minutes," he warned. "Tops. Then you have to be on your way."

"Great." Emily felt a completely uncalled-for fluttering in her middle. "You won't regret it."

THE TRUTH WAS, Dylan already regretted it. Emily McCabe might be all wrong for him, but she was also the kind of woman he could fall hard for. And the last thing either of them needed was any more complications in their already overburdened lives.

So on the drive over, he figured out how to get what needed

to be done accomplished in the shortest time possible so he could send her on her way.

He led the way in his pickup truck. She followed in her car. The first problem appeared as soon as they had parked and she got out of her sporty little sedan. He looked at her shoes. No question, her sandals were not appropriate for the pen.

Emily caught his gaze and lifted a hand. "Not to worry, cowboy. I've got that covered."

And to prove it, she sashayed back to the trunk and opened it up. Inside were enough clothes, shoes and purses to fill a closet. Deliberately, Emily fished out a pair of cowgirl boots.

"Come prepared, do you?" Dylan quipped, wondering if there was a toothbrush and nightie in there somewhere, too.

Emily shot him an arch look over her shoulder. "I'm a Texan, after all," she declared with a warm, winning smile.

She was so darn charming he couldn't help but smile back. "So naturally it follows…?"

She winked mischievously. "That I can't go anywhere without at least one pair of boots."

Dylan stood by while she bent to slip off her sandals. She donned a pair of socks and her cowgirl boots, the hem of her dress riding up her thighs as she did so.

Dylan ignored the immediate response of his body and headed for the barn. There, he switched on both interior and exterior lights, the yellow glow a beacon of reassurance in the moonlit, starry Texas night.

He came back with two bunches of alfalfa leaves.

As always, Emily was raring to go. "You always feed them this late?"

"They require up to fifteen-pound rations of hay per horse per day. Because of their small stomachs, it's better to feed and let them forage all day."

"Makes sense." Emily fell into step beside Dylan.

"And it's a way to rapidly increase their trust of me and now you."

The three horses were in a high wood-rail-sided paddock, linked by a fenced aisleway to the two round training pens—one with a roof, one without—on either end. From where the horses stood, they could see everything that was going on. Another schooling plus. By the time it got to be their turn, the mustangs knew what to expect. Which again, made it easier for all of them.

With the ease of someone who had grown up around horses, and loved them dearly, Emily followed Dylan into the paddock. "How invested are you in actually doing the naming?" she asked curiously.

"Not at all." Focused on the feeding, Dylan tore off leaves of alfalfa and put them just ahead of the trio of horses. Emily followed suit.

And so they went—dropping, moving on, dropping another two leaves, moving on—until finally the horses were following them.

Emily kept her voice low and calm. "Does that mean you'll let me do it?"

Dylan shrugged and replied before he could think, "If it makes you happy."

Emily chuckled in delight. "Oh…so you want me happy now…."

Dylan rolled his eyes. "Don't let it go to your head." Clearing his throat, he nodded toward their equine companions. "So back to the stars of the show…."

Emily regarded them carefully. "The three-year-old should be Ginger. The yearlings, Salt and Pepper."

Made sense. Dylan nodded. "I'll let the interested parties know." Finished, they stepped out of the paddock. As they strode toward the barn, Emily asked, "Do you have a horse of your own?"

Dylan slanted her a glance. "What do you think?"

"Can I meet him, too?"

Women didn't usually ask him that. But then, Dylan thought, the women he saw usually weren't interested in horses. "Sure," he said.

EMILY EXPECTED a stallion, from a thoroughbred bloodline. Instead, she found a brown-and-white quarter horse–thoroughbred mix that would likely have ended up who-knows-where had someone not stepped in and seen the potential. The gelding came closer to Emily. He stuck his head over the stall door, lowered his head and sniffed her hair, and then her face. Emily reached up to stroke his face as his warm breath ghosted over her. His eyes were alert but gentle, and she found his presence calming and reassuring. Emily took the apple Dylan handed her and presented it to his horse. "What's his name?"

"Hercules."

Able to feel the strength emanating from the horse's sleekly muscled build, Emily smiled. "It suits him." And the horse, who was anything but blue-blooded, suited Dylan.

Dylan offered Hercules a carrot. Hercules took it and luxuriated in a nose rub from Dylan, too.

Emily's heart warmed at the overwhelming affection between man and horse. She turned to Dylan. "How long have you been riding?"

"Since I was fifteen."

Unable to resist, she prodded a little more. "Did you grow up on a ranch?"

Once again, she thought, in the silence that followed her question, it was like trying to get information out of a spy sworn to secrecy. Finally, Dylan said, "No. I spent time on one later, and that's when I learned to ride."

"And realized your calling was horses."

"More or less." He looked at his watch.

"Yeah, yeah, I know," Emily grumbled good-naturedly. "Time's up. But not before I say goodbye to everyone." She headed for the paddock situated between the round pens and stood looking at the three mustangs. They were gathered together on the opposite side of the corral, ears moving, nostrils flexing, clearly relaxed.

Scattered among other paddocks and turnout sheds in the distance were other horses Dylan was working with. They all looked pleasantly settled and enjoying the warm spring night, too. Thinking how much she loved the peace and the tranquility of this ranch, Emily turned back to Dylan and let her enthusiasm be her guide. "When are you going to start training the mustangs?"

He lifted one large hand in an indolent manner. "I'm going to work with Salt and Pepper tomorrow morning."

As he spoke, Salt and Pepper approached them, one coming up on either side of them. First, they nosed the wooden rails and then eventually came over to Emily to investigate her. After several long moments, they put their heads on Emily's shoulders for a nuzzle.

These young ones weren't going to be that difficult to train, Emily thought, as she rubbed their faces and touched their manes. Already, they seemed used to people.

The three-year-old mare, on the other hand, was going to require more intensive schooling. Emily wanted to see how it was done. She turned to Dylan, watching as the two yearlings went over to greet him, too. "When will you work with Ginger?"

Dylan accepted their nuzzling with a grin. "Late afternoon, tomorrow."

Emily eyed the beautiful mare, who had moved closer but not close enough to touch. "Mind if I come and observe and maybe help a little?"

Dylan lifted a brow. "Sure you got time for that?"

It wasn't an invitation exactly, but it wasn't an edict to stay away, either. Emily smiled. "There's always time for something you want to do." And she really, really wanted to do this.

Chapter Five

"Looking at the Cowtown Diner is not going to make it disappear."

Guiltily, Emily moved away from the front window. Five more minutes, and the Daybreak Café would officially be closed. But with the exception of the tall, handsome cowboy standing next to her, it had been a ghost town for the past hour.

"There hasn't been a lull in the activity over there all day." Utility trucks had come and gone for gas, electricity, water and sewer. Safety inspections had been done, a neon light on the front of the diner turned on and tested.

Emily wanted to protest the burnished bronze exterior of the diner didn't fit in with the historic buildings on their side of the green, any more than proprietor Xavier Shillingsworth fit in Laramie. But the truth was the snazzy exterior and old-style-saloon design of the building added the kind of pizzazz that would have passing tourists stopping in droves.

Emily scowled. "There's a lot to do if they're going to open in two days."

Dylan laid a soothing hand on her shoulder. He leaned down to murmur in her ear, "You keep saying *if*."

Emily blew out a gusty breath. "Wishful thinking, I guess."

Dylan said matter-of-factly, "People are going to go there, to try it out and see what they think."

Their glances meshed. "You think I don't know that?" She turned away from the window and headed back to the booth Dylan had just vacated. She picked up his empty coffee cup and dessert plate and carried both to the kitchen.

Dylan ambled after her. "Once the newness wears off, they'll be back."

The point was, Emily didn't want to lose any customers in the first place. And really, how selfish was that?

Dylan was about to say something else, when the front door opened and slammed shut. Andrew walked in, book bag slung over his shoulder. "Mom!" he yelled.

Simone came out of the back.

Andrew thrust a paper at her. "I just got a job at the Cowtown Diner!"

Emily blinked in surprise.

"You already have a part-time job here," Simone reminded him.

Andrew shot her a look. "No offense, Miss Emily, but the diner is a much more awesome place to work. All my friends at school are getting jobs there. Everyone who works there has to be either in high school or college."

Or roughly Xavier's age, Emily thought, not sure whether that was a good or bad idea.

"So…can I?" Andrew asked his mom.

Emily looked at Simone. She did not want to put her friend on the spot. "Look, it's okay…"

"No," Simone said firmly, "it's not. Andrew, you have a part-time job here and you are going to honor that commitment."

A mother-son stare-down commenced.

Simone won.

"Fine!" Andrew slammed out the back.

An awkward silence followed.

"Sorry," Simone finally said, clearly upset.

"If you need to go ahead and leave for the day," Emily murmured sympathetically.

"Thanks…I think I will," Simone sighed, rushing out the back door.

Then things went from bad to worse.

The front door opened and Xavier Shillingsworth sauntered in.

How MUCH MORE was Emily supposed to have to take? Dylan wondered.

"Hi, Emily. Dylan—" Xavier paused dramatically. Furrowing his brow, he asked snidely, "—don't you ever work?"

Dylan refused to pick up the gauntlet. "You're not worth the effort, kid."

Disappointed, but no less smug, Xavier turned back to Emily. "Andrew's under sixteen so he's going to need a work permit. His mother will have to fill the papers out and get them approved by the Texas Workforce Commission, before he can start."

Emily continued wiping down tables. "They've already left for the day."

Shillingsworth followed her, further invading her space. "Maybe you could give the papers to them for me, then?"

Whatever pity he'd felt for the kid the previous evening vanished. Dylan stepped forward. "You know Andrew was working here?"

Shillingsworth lifted an autocratic brow. "Yes. He told me that."

Dylan studied him. "And you've got no compunction about trying to hire him away from Emily?"

"It's business. I'll hire anyone I want who wants a job. Even, say—" Xavier gestured lazily "—Emily…"

Oh, Dylan thought. *Them's fightin' words.*

Emily, on the other hand, stepped forward, fire in her gaze. "Well, kind as that is of you, Xavier," she drawled, "I really can't see that happening. Because I actually like to *cook* the food—from scratch—not just take off the plastic wrap and heat it in the microwave."

Dylan threw back his head and laughed. Having had more than enough, he slapped Xavier on the shoulder and steered him in the direction of the exit. He seemed to be doing that a lot. "Looks like you're outmatched and outclassed, kid. So you best be on your way."

Xavier stepped sideways instead. "First of all, you'd be surprised how good our stuff is." He squared off, indignant. "And second, Emily has not asked me to leave. So…"

Emily set her chin. "I'm asking you to leave."

Xavier looked at Emily, ready to continue to push the issue. Emily remained unmoved and Dylan lifted a warning brow.

The restaurateur suddenly changed his mind and headed slowly for the exit. "My offer of a date is good anytime, Emily. 'Cause I still want a cougar for my trophy case." The kid turned around and winked. "If you know what I mean."

Emily's glance narrowed. "Goodbye, Xavier."

Reluctantly, he sauntered out, slamming the door after him.

Emily turned to Dylan. Instead of complimenting him on the great restraint he had shown, in not booting the kid out by the seat of the pants practically the second the interloper walked in, Emily glared at him. "You do not have to run interference between the two of us. I am perfectly capable of looking after myself."

Dylan was willing to be amenable, but only to a point. "Suppose I want to defend you. Me being your pretend boy-friend and all. What then?"

He had no idea what Emily was going to say. He didn't

want to know, either. All he wanted, at that moment, was to stake his claim in a way neither of them would ever forget.

He wound an arm around her waist and used the leverage to pull her intimately against him. He heard her soft gasp of surprise—and delight—as he threaded his hand through her hair and tilted her face up to his.

The first contact was soft and tender. Their lips fused together. And yet there was no surrender.

It didn't matter.

Dylan had met with resistance before.

He knew gentleness and patience worked wonders.

As did a full-on kiss filled with passion and need.

He utilized both, grazing the shell of her ear, touching his mouth to her throat, the underside of her chin, her cheek, the tip of her nose, before moving once again to her lips.

And this time, when he fit his lips to hers in a soft, sure kiss, she was ready for him. Drawing him closer, she tangled her tongue with his….

The lines were blurring, Emily thought, as Dylan flattened a hand down her spine, pressing her body into his. Confusing her as to what was real and what wasn't…what was possible and what was not…

It didn't matter how hot and hard he was…or that she was the reason for it. It didn't matter that his embrace was magic, or that this fleeting embrace had her experiencing more pleasure than she ever had in her life.

What mattered was that they weren't in love.

Couldn't be.

Wouldn't be.

So even if it felt like something more, Emily told herself it wasn't.

Shaken, she broke off the kiss and pushed away. "This can't continue," she managed, drawing a jerky breath.

Not without some sort of promise that their relationship would one day be as real and true as the physical passion they felt.

Sadly, no matter how much he lusted after her, she couldn't see Dylan agreeing to that.

"I WASN'T SURE you'd show up," Dylan remarked when Emily got out of the car several hours later.

She had known he had figured no affair meant no working together, but she hadn't bothered to correct his misimpression at the time. "Then you must know even less about me than you think," Emily replied.

Dylan laughed and favored her with his sexy, oh-so-male presence and what-I'd-really-like-to-do-to-you golden-brown eyes.

She drew a conciliatory breath. "When I want to do something, I do it."

Dylan prodded devilishly. "And right now...?"

Emily settled her hat on her head. "I want to see you start Ginger's training."

Seeming pleased at that, Dylan dipped his head in a gallant bow and showed her the way. "Then let's get to it."

The horses Dylan was working with were housed in a maze of corrals and pastures, all feeding into a central alley. Salt and Pepper were in an adjacent paddock, grazing sedately. Ginger was by herself in another.

Dylan lifted the latch. Ginger took the opening he gave her and bolted down the aisleway. She took the first available exit and landed in a high-walled round pen. Dylan stepped in after her, closing the gate. Emily climbed onto the riser, above the pen, to watch.

"Easy, girl," Dylan said, as the beautiful mustang pranced back and forth, eyeing Dylan nervously all the while. He unfurled a long cloth line and gently threw it in the mare's direction. Ginger pranced away from it. Dylan pursued, calmly extending the line, forcing Ginger to go away from him again and again.

First in clockwise motion.

Then counterclockwise.

Across the center of the round pen.

Around the sides.

Again and again, they went.

"How long are you going to do this?" Emily asked.

Dylan cast her a look over his shoulder. He raised his hand—Ginger went faster. He dropped his hand to the side, she slowed. "Average time is about six minutes."

And then what? Emily wondered.

Six minutes later, she found out.

Dylan stopped throwing out the cloth line and simply stood quietly in the center of the pen. Slowly, he turned, so his shoulder was toward the mustang. Head bowed, he waited.

Ginger stood, trembling with nervousness.

Emily wondered what was up now.

Still, Dylan stood, his body quiet, posture relaxed, head down.

Ginger edged closer. Closer still, until her elegant thousand-pound body was right beside him.

Ever so slowly, Dylan turned toward her. Keeping his head down, his gaze on the ground, he murmured, "That's it, sweetheart. See? I'm not going to hurt you. I'm your friend."

With exquisite gentleness, he rubbed Ginger's face, then moved around to stroke the sides of her neck, her back, the vulnerable skin of her stomach, and back around to her hips and flanks. Emily watched, mesmerized, as the once-wild horse leaned into his touch, completely accepting, trusting absolutely.

"That was amazing," Emily said an hour later, when Dylan led the mustang back to the paddock where Salt and Pepper were pastured. So this was what horse whisperers did. "Do you use the same method every time?"

Dylan nodded, matter-of-fact in his expertise. "The horse has to go away from me before he or she can come back to me."

"So you drove her away repeatedly," Emily marveled. "And yet you knew she would come back to you in the end."

Dylan inclined his head. "It's basic horse—or herd—psychology."

To want what you can't have? To go where you're not supposed to be? "Or psychology in general." Emily paused. Suddenly suspicious as her next thought hit, she narrowed her eyes at Dylan. "So I have to ask—is that what you've been doing to me?"

DYLAN STARED at Emily, hoping the conversation wasn't headed where it appeared to be. "What are you talking about?" he demanded.

Emily gave Dylan a deliberately provoking look and smiled with all the steely resolve of a Texas belle, born and bred. "You pique my interest," she observed sweetly. Then she looked at him in a way that made him want to haul her into his arms and kiss her senseless. *Which maybe, given the heat between them, was not such a bad idea....*

Emily stepped closer yet and continued with a cantankerous toss of her head. "You only let me—or any other woman for that matter—come so close."

That was true of other women, he thought. Not Emily.

Her soft lips pursed in dismay. "Then you drive her away, again and again."

Once more, she seemed to be watching and weighing everything he said and did.

"Waiting patiently," Emily continued. "*Knowing* that she'll come back and join up with you in the end, just the way Ginger did."

If Dylan didn't know better, he would think it was Emily's heart that was hurting, instead of her pride. When the truth was, this was about something much more fundamental. He folded his arms and leaned against the fence. "You're making it too complicated," he said mildly.

She brushed past him, a censuring light in her eyes, a downward slant to her lips. "I don't think so."

He caught her by the arm and swung them both around so fast she stumbled into his chest. His own body humming with the crazy feeling of need running riot inside him, he steadied her, then planted his hands on either side of her and leaned over her, so she was pinned between his body and the smooth rails of the wooden fence.

He let his eyes slide over the inviting curves of her breasts, flat abdomen and sexy, jean-clad legs, before returning to her tousled hair, soft lips and wide blue eyes. "There's nothing complicated about me wanting you, or what I need," he told her frankly, not afraid to be bold if boldness was what was called for.

She released a breath. "Which is what exactly?"

Ignoring the flash of indignation on her pretty face, Dylan leaned even closer. He'd lost the battle to be a gentleman, but if nothing else, he would be honest. "To take you in my arms," he said very, very softly, "and make love to you."

Before Emily could do more than gasp, Dylan caught her beneath the knees, swung her up into his arms and strode toward the house. Resenting having his integrity and his actions questioned now—especially by Emily, who had spent enough time with him to know better—Dylan continued acting with the total freedom he'd enjoyed his entire adult life.

"What's complicated," he told her, as he mounted the steps

and carried her on into the house, "is the notion of us being together."

His point made, that if they so chose, the two of them could do anything they damn well wanted, he set her down inside the foyer.

Not sure when he had ever been so thoroughly exasperated by a woman, he gazed at her. "'Cause there is no way you're ever going to want what I want—a no-strings affair that lasts as long as we want it to and still allows us to walk away, completely unscathed."

And that was one heck of a shame….

Sparks gleamed in Emily's blue eyes. "Want to bet?" she challenged.

DYLAN THOUGHT she was a chicken. That she'd never be wild and reckless and yes—*courageous*—enough to act on the needs of her body. He was wrong. And she was going to show him.

Giving him no chance to resist, Emily bounded up and leaped into his arms. She landed with her arms wrapped around his neck and shoulders, her legs locked around his waist.

Caught completely by surprise, Dylan stumbled backward, his weight falling against the wall. And then all was lost in the first thrilling rush of freedom and the impact of her lips planted squarely on his. Emily knew he didn't mean to kiss her back. Any more than she could help kissing him. And somehow that made the culmination of their mutual desire all the hotter.

This wasn't supposed to happen.

Yet it was.

She wasn't supposed to be this reckless.

Yet she was.

"Emily. Emily…" Dylan groaned.

The rush of emotion overwhelmed her. In the feminine heart of her, the tingling started. "Don't stop." She caught his face in her hands, looked deep into his eyes and whispered, "Don't stop." She celebrated the victory of being together, of leaving constraints behind. Of daring intimacy…and sex… and the possibility that every fantasy she had about him just might come true…

And he seemed enthralled, too. He deepened the kiss, exploring her mouth with his tongue, leaving not a millimeter untouched. Sensation swept through her like a tsunami, followed by a tidal wave of need. It had been so long since she had been held and kissed with anywhere near this conviction. Never mind the pure physical need.

When his hand slipped beneath her blouse and cupped her breast through the lace of her bra, Emily arched her back and trembled with pleasure. She was drowning in the incredible sensations sweeping through her. Wanting more, Emily threaded her hands through his hair and held his head. "Let's go to bed, Dylan," she whispered, her breath coming raggedly. "Right now."

Dylan paused, breathing hard. Clearly he wanted to take their lovemaking to the limit and beyond. He searched her face. "You're sure?"

"Very."

His glance dropped to the nipples protruding visibly through her blouse. He flashed her a debilitating sexy grin. His grip tightening possessively, he regarded her with a mock gallantry that kindled her senses. "Well, then, whatever the lady wants…"

He shifted her closer to his chest and carried her, still straddling his waist, through the hall and up the steps. He strode down the hall and lowered her, with surprising gentleness, onto the rumpled covers of his bed. Pausing only long enough to kick off his boots and take off hers, he stretched out next to her.

She flushed hotly as he unbuttoned her blouse, dropping kisses along the curve of her cheek, the slope of her neck, the décolletage of her bra. He looked at her lovingly as he traced the bow shape of her lips with his fingertip.

Then that, too, dropped to her breast.

He found the curve, the tip, the valley in between. Emily shuddered in response. She had never felt more beautiful than she did at that moment, seeing herself reflected in his gaze. "I knew we'd end up together," he whispered, kissing her again, desire exploding through them in liquid, melting heat.

Then he was on top of her, his weight as welcoming as a blanket on a cold winter's night, his mouth on hers in a kiss that was shattering in its seductive sensuality. He kissed her as if he were in love with her, and would be for all time. He kissed her as if he had always known they had something special and were meant to be together like this.

Emily had never before felt such deep-seated longing surge through her, driving her toward wild abandon. And these intoxicating emotions proved to be the ultimate aphrodisiac.

Feeling sexier, more adventurous than she had in her entire life, she gave herself over to the experience. Moaning softly as Dylan unclasped her bra and explored the tenderness of her skin. She arched in ecstasy with each caress of hand and lips and tongue. Then she unbuttoned his shirt and discovered the hard masculine contours of his chest. Lower still, she unzipped his jeans, releasing the burgeoning proof of his desire.

He was hot and hard all over. All warm satin skin and coarse wheat-blond hair. Determined to prove to him that she was as exciting and fiercely independent as he was, she held his eyes with the promise of the hot, languid lovemaking to come....

DYLAN HADN'T MEANT for any of this to happen.

He *had* expected to spend time with her. Maybe put on a little show of public ardor once or twice, do whatever it was she felt "couples" did together, until the facade ended.

But that was before he had watched her dare damn near everything and luxuriated in the soft, silky feel of her. Or looked into the turbulent sea-blue of her eyes and kissed her hard and soft and every way in between.

"You've got to promise me something," he whispered, as he took her to the very edge of the bed. The need to make her his was stronger than ever. "No heartache. No regrets…"

"Just pleasure," she whispered back, "in the here and now."

And those vows were all it took, Dylan noted, to get her on the same track as he. She moaned against him, kissing him ardently. Even as she surrendered, she took. Even as he gave, he found.

Determined to set the pace, he parted her legs and slipped between her thighs. Holding her close, he pushed inside her, timing his movements as she wrapped her limbs around him and lifted her body to his.

His hands caught her hips as she pulled him deeper still. Their eyes locked and a mixture of tenderness and primal possessiveness filled his soul. He knew it was just friendship and sex, but it felt like more. Although he knew it would end, it felt like it never would. And then there was no more prolonging the inevitable. Trembling, they succumbed to the swirling, enviable pleasure.

EMILY LAY CUDDLED in Dylan's strong arms for long moments afterward, still hardly able to believe what had happened. It was just sex. They'd both been very clear about that. Yet…the magic of his tender, amazing lovemaking left her feeling that Dylan intuitively understood what she wanted and needed in a way no one else ever had, or would. And that left her feeling oddly weak and susceptible.

Odds were, *vulnerable* was not what Dylan wanted to see from her. Hence, this was her chance to prove how detached she could be, too. Adopting a studied, casual look, she extricated herself from his warm embrace, rose and began to dress.

As always, Dylan saw way more than she would have preferred. He lay where he was, arms folded behind his head, seeming to intuit her emotions were in turmoil, even though his expression was inscrutable, too. "What are you thinking?" he asked finally, his voice as casual as her demeanor.

Searching for a decidedly flip remark, Emily shrugged. "The obvious." She flashed a flirtatious grin. "That you're not just a horse whisperer. You're a woman whisperer, too."

His eyes crinkled at the corners, her backhanded compliment only partially satisfying him. He regarded her with rueful contemplation, something hot and sensual shimmering in his eyes. "This is going to be a problem, isn't it?"

His husky voice sent shivers down her spine.

Emily glanced down and realized she had buttoned her shirt incorrectly. Dismayed by the evidence of her disquiet, she opened the fastenings and started all over again. "I don't know what you mean." Her fingers trembled as much as her voice.

He threw back the covers and walked toward her in all his naked glory. "You're not the kind of woman who can get involved with someone or have an affair without asking them to commit to something for a lot longer term—and to change into what you need them to be."

Emily sent him the kind of offhand glance meant to presage a quick and uncomplicated exit. She moved away. "That's not true."

"I think it is." He sauntered closer, studying the turbulent emotion in her eyes. "I think you're waiting for some guy to come in and let you change him as much as you want, without demanding anything of you in return. And the two of you will marry and live happily ever after."

Emily kept her eyes above the waist. "I don't think that way!"

He shook his head. "The look on your face just now says otherwise."

More attracted to him than ever, Emily wiggled into her jeans. "I admit, I've never had an out-and-out fling before."

Dylan pulled on his clothes and boots. He gave her the same look her parents gave her when they thought she needed to delve deeper into the workings of her heart. "How many boyfriends have you had?"

Emily picked up his brush and ran it through her hair. "Casual?" *Meaning the kind she left with a kiss, at the door?* "Tons."

He frowned. "Serious."

Emily sighed. "Two. One in college. One about four years ago."

Dylan took her hand and led her toward the hall. "What happened?"

Emily followed him down the stairs. "The first one felt it was his duty as my significant other to try and control me."

Dylan let go of her hand as they wandered into the kitchen. "I bet that went over well."

"You can only imagine," Emily admitted drily.

He looked in the fridge. "And the second?"

Emily lounged against the counter, observing the enticing play of muscles in his chest and shoulders beneath his shirt. Within her, desire started all over again.

Forcing herself to keep her mind on the conversation, she replied, "He couldn't get along with my family."

He set a smoked chicken from Sonny's Barbeque on the counter. Added flour tortillas and a hunk of Colby-Jack. "Why not?"

Curious—because she had assumed Dylan couldn't cook—Emily moved back to give him room to work. "Ridge liked his family better. He thought they were superior to mine, and he wanted us to spend all our time—every holiday and a lot of other weekends, as well—with them."

Dylan added olive oil to a cast-iron skillet. "Doesn't sound fair."

"It wasn't." Emily paced while Dylan chopped up an onion and green pepper and added those to the skillet, too. "I tried to get Ridge to be reasonable about the situation—to at least divide the extended-family time fifty-fifty, but he wouldn't budge, so that ended that." The kitchen quickly filled with a delicious aroma.

"And since then…"

"There's been no one serious." Emily hadn't wanted to get hurt. "I haven't wanted to put myself out there, emotionally, unless I knew everything else was falling into line, that we were going to be compatible in all the ways that mattered, even if that meant one…or both of us…had to change."

Dylan wrapped the tortillas in foil and set them in the oven to heat. "And you were willing to do that," he murmured, as he grated the cheese.

Emily nodded. "Sometimes the guys were, too. But ultimately, that didn't work, either, because if you have to make yourself over to be with someone…you sort of start questioning if it's worth it."

Dylan brought out some premade guacamole, pico de gallo and sour cream. "I can understand that."

"Anyway, I got frustrated with working so hard on a personal life and failing, so two years ago I decided to start pouring all my energy into my career."

Dylan added smoked chicken to the sizzling vegetables. "And that's when you started the café."

Emily nodded, edging closer to the stove. She watched as he gave the ingredients a stir. "And then, it became my baby," she said softly. "So to speak."

Dylan brought out two bottles of cold dark beer. Emily set the table. Minutes later, they sat down to eat their smoked-chicken tacos. Emily was pleased to find the pulled-together feast was every bit as delicious as it looked.

Deciding to satisfy her curiosity as well as her appetite, Emily murmured eventually, "Okay, enough of a confessional from me. What is your romantic history like? Have you ever been head over heels in love?"

Dylan paused. "I thought I was at the time. Looking back, I'm not so sure."

"What happened?"

"I was working on a horse ranch in Wyoming, and I fell hard for the boss's daughter. Mariah was in college at the time. I only had my GED. She knew her parents wouldn't approve, so we had to see each other on the sly."

This did not sound good.

"She kept telling me that it would be all right once she finished her undergrad and got into vet school—that her parents would know she wasn't going to give up on her dream to be with me."

"But it wasn't," Emily guessed.

Dylan shook his head. "In her parents' view, a line had been crossed. There is the hired help—"

"You."

"And the rest of the cowboys and house staff. And then there is the landowner. In their view I was never going to be part of the latter."

That had to have hurt. "Did they fire you?"

Dylan nodded. "Oh, yeah, and they refused to give me a

recommendation, which made it hard as hell to get another job—at least a good one—for a while."

"I see," she murmured. "Employers want to know why you left."

His face hardened. "I wasn't going to lie."

"But at the same time…"

"When you say you had to leave because of an unfortunate romantic entanglement with the boss's daughter, it doesn't look good." He exhaled sharply. "And you can forget it, if the prospective employer has a daughter of courting age."

"Which brings us back to that talk you had with my father…" she prompted gently.

Guilt flashed across Dylan's handsome face.

Emily leaned toward him. "He wanted to know what your intentions were, didn't he?"

Dylan's expression grew cagey. "He didn't put it like that."

"But he said something in the vicinity."

Dylan lifted an infuriatingly autocratic hand. "You don't need to worry about it."

"But I—" Emily stopped abruptly at the sound of high-pitched whinnying. "Dylan, did you hear that?" she asked in alarm.

"Yes." Dylan rose. "I sure as heck did."

Chapter Six

Emily and Dylan rushed out to find Andrew letting himself into the paddock with the three wild mustangs.

"Let 'em all out!" the rowdy boys shouted.

"Andrew, no!" Emily screamed.

Realizing they were busted, the three teenage boys on the outside of the corral left Andrew high and dry and bolted for the pickup truck in the driveway. Dylan and Emily made no move to stop them as they peeled out—their concern was for the trapped, shaking boy, and the three horses who sensed danger.

"Easy, now, Ginger." Dylan entered the enclosure. Head bowed, Dylan turned his shoulder toward the mare and tried to draw her in. She was having none of it. Her eyes were on the quaking boy behind him. Emily opened the gate, moving slowly and quickly, and slid inside, too.

While Dylan talked to the mustangs, urging Salt and Pepper to stay calm, Emily grabbed a hold of Andrew's arm. She guided him outside the corral and shut the gate behind them.

Dylan continued soothing the three mustangs. When all were calm, he eased out of the gate and strode toward Emily and Andrew.

"Keep him here," Dylan ordered before striding into the house.

Embarrassed and surly, Andrew yelled, "Go ahead—call my mom. I don't care."

What had happened to the once-sweet boy, Emily wondered. Who was this angry, defiant stranger?

Andrew wheeled on her. "Maybe you'll fire me from the café now, too."

"Is that what you want?" Emily asked, shocked.

"I want to do what I want, when I want."

"Andrew, you're only fifteen. You don't want to start doing things that will earn you a criminal record."

Andrew shrugged. "Maybe it's in my blood. Maybe I'm just like my dad," he asserted, as Dylan returned. "Maybe I belong in jail, too."

Was that what this was about? Emily shot a troubled look at Dylan.

Andrew glared at Dylan. "I don't know what the big deal is," he said angrily. "I didn't really do anything."

"You were trespassing, and you could have been killed," Dylan reprimanded sternly. "That's plenty."

Andrew fumed. "What did my mom say? Is she coming to get me?"

"I didn't speak with her." Dylan looked at Andrew without apology. "I spoke with the sheriff's department. They have a patrol car in the area. Deputy Rio Vasquez will be here momentarily to take you into custody."

Custody! "Was that really necessary?" Emily asked Dylan, after Andrew had been cuffed, read his rights and taken to the station.

"What would you have had me do?" Dylan stalked back into the ranch house, as impatient with her as she was with him.

"You should have called Simone!"

"The sheriff's department can do that." Dylan shoved his wallet in the back pocket of his jeans and picked up his keys.

Emily followed him out to the pickup truck.

"This could have been handled privately."

Dylan disagreed. "If we don't hold him accountable, all this will be is a close call and an incentive to do more the next time."

Dylan caught her by the shoulders and continued before she could interrupt, "And make no mistake about it, Emily, there will be a next time—unless something happens to shake some sense into Andrew and get him off this path."

Her emotions in turmoil, Emily glared at Dylan. "What makes you so sure of that? Maybe what happened tonight is the wake-up call Andrew needs, to straighten up."

Dylan let go of her, and stepped back. "I'm not changing my mind, Emily."

She thought of all the devastation Simone had been through the past couple of years, first with the shock of her husband being arrested for masterminding a burglary ring and sent to jail, the resultant divorce, and now Andrew's incessant "attitude" and rebellion. Surely, Simone didn't deserve to relive the nightmare of her husband's tangles with the law, with her only son. "Not even if I beg you to reconsider, for the sake of my friends?" Emily asked plaintively.

Dylan shook his head. "Not even then."

"I'VE NEVER SEEN IT so deserted in here," Hank remarked, when he came into the café the next morning, accompanied by a debonair gentleman she didn't recognize.

Emily looked at her older brother. Since he'd gotten married, the ex-Marine had become as hopelessly romantic as their parents. Like Greta and Shane, Hank wanted to see everyone he loved happily paired up. Unfortunately, Emily thought, thinking back to her own love life—or sudden lack thereof—such a fate was not in the cards for everyone. Especially not her and Dylan Reeves, the spectacular sex they'd had notwithstanding…

"The Cowtown Diner is having its grand opening this morning," Emily explained.

"Yeah," Hank commiserated. "The line was around the block when the doors opened at six this morning."

Emily bristled, the betrayal she felt as unexpected as it was intense. "Did you and Ally eat there?" she asked her older brother.

Hank frowned. "Of course not. But I probably will at some point. Got to support all the businesses in town, you know. And speaking of business…I'd like you to meet Aaron Markham. He's a tax attorney and CPA from Dallas."

Emily welcomed the nice-looking man in the gray suit. "Nice to meet you."

"Since you're not busy, maybe you could sit down for a few minutes and chat with us," Hank suggested.

"How about I bring you-all some coffee and a few menus first?" Emily suggested.

She gave them their choice of tables and hurried off.

Aaron Markham seemed like a pleasant and personable man. Her brother meant well. She could not have been less interested.

Until the door to the café opened and closed and Dylan Reeves walked in, that was.

Their eyes locked.

Emily felt a thrill go through her, followed swiftly by anger.

She carried the coffeepot over to the table. Hank tracked the direction of her gaze. "Yeah…" he murmured. "I heard what happened at Dylan's ranch last night."

"Then you also know how wrong he was!" Not waiting for her brother's take on the situation, Emily stalked over to Dylan's table. "A word with you, please?"

Dylan gestured to the other side of the booth. "Have a seat."

He only wished she were that malleable! Emily gritted her teeth. "I'd prefer to take this outside."

Dylan rose with exaggerated chivalry. "After you."

Emily ushered the incorrigible rancher through the back door, into the alley. She didn't know why she was still so angry with Dylan. She had disagreed with others plenty of times, on a variety of subjects, and never been this emotional, but somehow this felt intensely personal. As if she should have been able to talk to him and effect some change. Instead, he'd been as immovable as a two-ton boulder and, from the looks of it, still was.

"Simone had to post bail last night to get Andrew out of jail," Emily reported.

"It might have been better had she let him stay the night in a cell."

She should have known Dylan would say that, Emily thought, with quickly mounting aggravation. And when had he gotten to be such a hard case?

Emily huffed and went on, "The arraignment was held this morning. Thanks to your statement and the recommendation of the sheriff's department, the district attorney charged Andrew—and his three accomplices—with trespassing and third-degree burglary. His friends all had previous records and have been sent to juvenile detention. Only Andrew, thus far, has been released to parental custody. And rather than be relieved, he was resentful about that, too." Emily paused, shook her head. "I've never seen Simone so upset." She had told her to take a few days off—with pay—until she could get things straightened out.

Dylan listened quietly. "How's Andrew taking it?" he asked finally.

"He's angry and ashamed."

"Remorseful?" he pressed.

"I wouldn't say that."

Dylan nodded, not at all surprised.

Where was his compassion? Emily wondered in frustration. She knew he had it—he showed it to the horses he trained. He'd also bestowed it on her on more than one occasion.

"And don't say *I told you so,*" Emily grumbled, actually as shocked as Simone that the trauma of being arrested hadn't been enough to shake some sense into the fifteen-year-old boy.

Something inscrutable flickered in Dylan's expression as he folded his arms across his chest. "I wasn't planning on it."

Emily studied Dylan, not about to let him off the hook for his part in this mess.

For a moment she thought he was going to put up the usual barrier to his private thoughts. Instead, something in his gaze shifted, became more intimate which, in turn, prompted her to admit, "I'm afraid this is going to backfire on everyone." Emily sighed. "That all it will do is make a bad situation worse."

"That's up to Andrew."

Emily wasn't used to feeling this helpless. She wrung her hands. "I feel I should do something."

Dylan placed a steadying hand on her elbow. "The best thing you can do is stand back and let it play out. This is Andrew's life. These are his choices to make, his consequences to deal with."

Emily forced herself to remain calm. "He hasn't made the right choices thus far," she warned.

"Let's hope that changes," Dylan said. "And soon."

EMILY WAS NOT CONTENT to leave everything up to fate—or the impulsive emotions of a teenage boy in crisis. As soon as the café closed for the day, she drove over to the sheriff's department, to see what she could do.

Luck was with her. Deputy Rio Vasquez, the officer who'd arrested Andrew the night before, was just coming on duty. Her cousin, Kyle McCabe, was also on shift.

The two deputies shared the same outlook. "Dylan was right to call us and take a hard line," Rio said.

Kyle nodded. "I know it seems like it isn't that big a deal. But it is. Pranks like this are gateway crimes. The kids don't see it that way, of course. They think they're just messing around and accepting dares and having fun." He sighed heavily. "But things have a way of getting out of control—fast—with kids this age and before you know it, someone is badly hurt. Or there's a fatal car accident. And then lives are really turned upside down."

"Dylan knows this better than anyone," Rio added.

Emily did a double take. "What do you mean?" she asked.

Rio and Kyle exchanged wary looks.

Whatever they knew, Emily realized in disappointment, they weren't going to share.

"The point is," Rio continued, sidestepping her question completely, "Dylan takes the situation very seriously. And that's good. The worst thing any of you could have done is used your influence with the district attorney to try to have the whole matter dropped, before any real consequences were felt."

Dylan had said as much, but somehow it helped hearing the same thing from two such experienced lawmen.

Emily thanked them both, and Kyle walked her outside. Because he was her cousin, and they'd grown up together, he knew her pretty well. "So does this mean it's over with you and Dylan Reeves?" he asked curiously.

Emily could confide in Kyle the way she couldn't confide

in her brothers. "I don't know. I'm not sure I could date anyone who is as intractable as he is, for very long." Maybe it would be best to cut her losses while the potential damage to her heart was still small.

"So it's not like the two of you are in love or anything?" Kyle teased.

Emily blushed. "Heavens, no!"

"You were just kissing him on the green, the other night…."

"You saw that?"

"Emily, everyone saw that. It looked pretty hot."

It had been hot. Their tumble into bed the evening before, hotter still. But sex wasn't everything. Even between friends. Emily bit her lip. "I'm just not sure we're compatible in the ways that count."

Kyle chuckled. "You mean he's not makeover material."

"I haven't tried to make him over." Not like she had in the past. She hadn't gone clothes shopping with him, helped decorate his place or suggested a way to further his career aspirations—like she had with the previous guys she had dated….

Clearly not seeing the difference in her approach to this male-female relationship, Kyle lifted a skeptical brow. "Well, that's good. Because unlike your previous boyfriends—who, by the way, were all way too malleable for their own good— Dylan is a man who operates on the strength of his convictions. And I don't see that changing. Not for you. Not for anyone."

EMILY HAD PROMISED herself she would not get enmeshed in any more dead-end romances. Which left her with only one choice.

"I think we should be friends," she told Dylan, when she showed up at his ranch that afternoon.

"I thought we already were. Or at least were on the way to becoming good friends."

"What I mean is," Emily explained, aware her voice sounded a little rusty, and her emotions felt all out of whack, too, "I don't think we should have sex again."

Their glances locked and they shared another moment of tingling awareness. Finally, Dylan said, "It was that bad, hmm?"

Emily told herself not to read anything into the concern in his eyes. "You know it wasn't," she murmured, blushing. The truth was she had climaxed like crazy under his masterful touch. "But sex complicates things. I don't need additional complications right now. My life is chaotic enough."

Dylan rocked back on his heels. He tore off his leather work gloves and braced his hands on his hips. "Okay."

Emily tore her gaze from his rock-solid chest and abs. She looked into his eyes, a little surprised he hadn't argued with her. She cleared her throat. "You're fine with this?"

The tension between Dylan's shoulder blades eased. "You just told me no. I respect that, and I will honor that." His gaze gentling all the more, he flashed her a crooked smile meant to conciliate. He stepped closer and lifted a hand to her cheek, briefly touching the side of her face. "That doesn't mean I still don't want to have sex with you. So," he said, and slanted her a telling look, "if you change your mind and decide you would like to have sex with me again, it's up to you to let me know."

Emily wasn't used to guys being this reasonable. Aware her face was still tingling from his brief, sensual touch, she drew a deep breath. "Okay, then."

"Okay." Another pause. He scanned her Western-wear-clad form. "Did you want to help with the mustangs?" he asked finally, as cheerful as ever when it came to his work.

Emily smiled, glad her efforts to redirect their relationship had worked out so well. "I would love to."

Dylan turned and headed for the training area. "Salt and Pepper have already been put through paces today."

Falling into step beside him, Emily teased, "Saving the best for last?"

Dylan winked. "I figured you would show up, and since Ginger clearly is your favorite…" He walked into the round pen, motioning for Emily to join him.

This time, when he shut the gate, Ginger came right over to him. Everywhere Dylan went, the mustang followed. He petted her nose, her mane, her neck. Ran a hand under her abdomen, across her flanks and down her legs. The beautiful mare seemed to not just tolerate his handling of her, but welcome it.

A phenomenon Emily understood all too well…

"I noticed you're not disagreeing with my assessment that you've been playing favorites with the herd," Dylan said.

Flushing with guilt, Emily shrugged. "What can I say? Ginger's complicated and challenging. I'm trying to understand her."

Dylan nodded his agreement, looking as if that was a conundrum *he* understood all too well. "The question is, will she *allow* us to tame her?"

"What do you mean?" Emily watched rancher and horse interact with teamlike proficiency. "It's been less than a week and Ginger is already following you around the pen, going wherever you go…."

"You're right, she is watching my every move. Unfortunately, her curiosity is more than a demonstration of interest— it's an expression of fear." He met her eyes. "A horse doesn't bother to investigate something that it is not afraid of. A horse isn't curious unless it harbors some uncertainty. And that underlying fear can make a horse unpredictable."

Emily watched Dylan pick up one hoof. Ginger bucked slightly and wrested her leg from his light, testing grasp.

Dylan went back to stroking Ginger all over. When she was calm, he tried again, picking up her foot. Again, she resisted but he didn't back down.

And on and on it went, until at last Ginger gave in and let Dylan touch and rub and inspect all four feet without complaint.

"Now you try," Dylan said, while holding on to the lightweight training halter on Ginger's head.

Emily—whose only experience had been with the tame-from-birth quarter horses her father bred and trained—moved away from the wall.

Ginger eyed Emily warily while Dylan murmured soothingly and stroked her face. She pricked her ears and lifted her head slightly, inspecting Emily with her dark, soulful eyes. She seemed to be waiting to see if she could trust Emily as much as Dylan.

Emily took her time, just as Dylan had. Murmuring softly, she explained every step she took, every move she made. Ginger reacted in kind, calmly allowing Emily to pet her all over. Then finally, tenderly nosing Emily's hands, before gently nuzzling her face.

"I think she's in love," Dylan said softly.

I think I could be in love, Emily thought. *With both of you. If I were foolish, that is. Good thing I'm not.*

The mustang wasn't hers to keep, and neither was Dylan. Ginger had a home to go to—when she was trained. Dylan already had a home of his own; he'd made it clear for years now that he didn't want to share it with anyone.

Nothing about that seemed to have changed.

Emily shrugged off the compliment. "She knows kindness when she sees it."

Dylan slipped outside the gate and came back with two apples. He tossed them to Emily. "Reward her."

She did.

Dylan returned Ginger to the paddock with Salt and Pepper, then strode back, praise in his eyes. "Now it's time for me to reward you," he said, flashing her a sexy grin.

Emily knew what quickly sprang to *her* mind, despite their new just-friends status. Afraid she would get herself in just as deep as she had the night before if she didn't watch it, she warned herself to slow down. She put up a staying hand. "You really don't have to do that, Dylan. Just being able to spend time with Ginger is thanks enough."

"You don't want to owe anyone anything? I don't want to be beholden to anyone, either." He looked at her, his mind clearly made up. "So I'm taking you to dinner as payment. It's up to you to say when and where."

Chapter Seven

Dylan waited while Emily stood, tapping her foot and considering her options. "Tonight. The Cowtown Diner."

Where she was likely to run into Xavier Shillingsworth again? "You're joking," Dylan said mildly.

Her expression innocent, Emily swept off her hat and ran her fingers through her silky locks. "I figure we should be neighborly. And since you're paying…"

Dylan knew trouble brewing when he saw it. "I think it's a dumb idea," he said bluntly.

"Really." She plopped her hat back on her head and shot him a sassy look, determined to do what she wanted no matter what he thought. "How so?"

"Tonight is the grand opening for the dinner rush."

"So?" Her lower lip slid out in a sexy pout.

"So we're likely to have to wait for a table," he said.

Emily shrugged. "I'm okay with that. The only thing is, I want to go home and shower first."

Dylan was the first to admit he needed to do the same. "You want me to pick you up?"

She nodded. "Seven-thirty okay with you?"

"Fine with me."

It was the rest of the evening he wondered about.

DYLAN WASN'T SURE what he had expected Emily's apartment to look like inside. The glimpse he'd had of the adjacent bath and bedroom revealed a pink and frilly décor. This surprised him, because he'd never seen her wear anything pink or frilly, since he'd been in town.

The living area where he sat was a lot more predictable. She had a large overstuffed ivory sofa and a pair of mismatched wing chairs. Blinds, but no drapes. There were a lot of throw pillows in different fabrics and sizes. A couple of throws—one in burgundy velour, the other a soft sage-green knit. Nice lamps. And one wall that was all bookshelves, filled with fiction, cookbooks and horse stories.

An antique leather-and-brass steamer trunk served as her coffee table. Cooking magazines, especially ones that featured Southwestern-style cooking, were piled high. A small round table and two chairs and a kitchenette that could only be described as woefully inadequate. It didn't even have a stove or microwave, just a hot plate, sink and dorm-size fridge.

Emily swept back out, shutting the bedroom door behind her. But not before he'd caught sight of the wardrobe crisis that had just ensued. There were clothes scattered everywhere.

He liked the ones she had on, though.

Emily strode toward the kitchen counter and snatched up her purse and keys. She spun around in a drift of floral perfume. "Ready to go?"

Ready for something...that's for sure, Dylan thought, feeling an uncomfortable pressure at the front of his jeans.

To distract himself, he let his glance sift over her pretty turquoise dress and surprisingly high heels. Damn, but she had a nice body. Nice legs, too.

"You look good," he said gruffly. "Too good to be eating in an unscrupulous competitor's restaurant."

Her soft lips curved in a parody of a smile. "Thanks. I think."

Resisting the urge to pull her close and kiss her again, he

said, "You know Shillingsworth is probably going to conclude you dressed up just for him."

Emily's brow arched. "Then he would be wrong—you're my date. Not that I dressed up for you," she amended quickly. "I dressed up for me. Because I like to look nice when I go out."

He studied the rosy color in her cheeks, the emotion shimmering in her eyes. "Well, you look gussied-up, all right."

Her gaze swept over his cleaned-up form, making him glad he had taken the time to iron his shirt and polish his boots, instead of just showering, shaving and finding a clean change of clothes. "So do you," she said softly.

Basking in the compliment, Dylan followed her down the stairs and into the alley behind the row of historic buildings downtown. On the other side of it was a row of slanted parking. Emily's car was there, beside his pickup truck.

Instead of going toward the passenger side of the truck, she hesitated and looked up at him. The last of the day's sunshine glimmered in her molasses-colored hair. He had to fight the urge to reach out and touch the soft, silky strands. "Want to walk or drive?"

"It's a nice evening." She caught his gaze. "It's only a couple of blocks. How about we hoof it?"

Anything to ease the pressure in the front of his jeans. "Sounds good."

She fell into step beside him.

He observed the pulse throbbing in her throat. "I've got a question."

"Fire away."

"This evening, are we still pretending we're dating? Or are we now publicly owning up to being 'just friends'?"

Her lips compressed. "Good question, since only one of my brothers has produced a potential love interest for me thus far, and my parents have ceased and desisted their matchmaking efforts entirely since we allegedly became a pair."

"Want my advice?" Dylan asked.

She cocked her head to one side and waited.

"Unless some gal has come in and swept Shillingsworth off his feet in the past twenty four hours or so, I very much doubt the little twerp has given up on making you his cougar."

She elbowed him gently. "Careful, cowboy, you're sounding a mite jealous."

"Not jealous," Dylan corrected. "Matter-of-fact. And I'll lay odds Shillingsworth makes another pass at you tonight, whether he thinks I'm your date or not."

Emily chuckled. "Enough to wager?"

"Depends on what the stakes are."

"One home-cooked meal. Cleanup, included."

Which meant another night alone together, wise or not. Dylan extended his hand. "Okay," he said agreeably. "You're on.…"

THE PLACE WAS HOPPING, when Emily and Dylan reached the newest dining establishment in town. Throngs of people stood in a line that filled the old-fashioned, saloon-style porch and extended halfway down the block, and more were arriving even as Dylan and Emily joined the line. And the patrons weren't just residents of Laramie. Emily garnered from the bits of conversation floating around, they were flocking in from all around the county.

And why not? The Cowtown Diner oozed excitement.

Exterior speakers played popular country and western music. A waitstaff of college- and high-school-age kids kept tabs on the activity with wireless headsets, while less experienced staff circulated among the waiting area with platters of free appetizers and tumblers of lemonade, water and iced tea.

Despite herself, Emily was impressed.

Maybe Xavier Shillingsworth knew a lot more than she thought he did.

Maybe age wasn't the defining factor so much as vision. And, Emily had to reluctantly admit, Xavier had taken the ordinary visage of a franchise-restaurant into a definite step above.

"Jalapeño poppers?" asked a pretty young girl, in a short burnt-orange cowgirl uniform and boots.

Emily and Dylan thanked her and helped themselves. He leaned down to whisper in her ear, "Not as good as yours."

It wasn't. "But darn close," Emily whispered back.

If not for the faint aftertaste of frozen batter on her rival's hors d'oeuvre, it would have been a tie.

"Hey, Emily!" Without warning, Xavier zipped down to join them on the sidewalk. He nodded at her date. "Hey, there, Devon."

"It's Dylan," Emily corrected.

Dylan locked eyes with Xavier. "Nice job on all this," he said politely.

Xavier seemed taken aback by the sincerity of Dylan's compliment. "Uh, thanks. Why don't you two come with me?"

He headed off, pushing his way past the line, leaving Emily to follow. Dylan was right behind her.

She expected Xavier to show them the restaurant kitchen. She wasn't expecting their host to cut through the line and place them at the next available table, an oversize booth that clearly could have sat six. "Whatever you want, it's on the house," he told them, while the people they had bypassed grumbled unhappily.

"Not cool," Emily sighed.

Dylan nodded, but said nothing.

A waiter appeared with a menu that was twice as extensive

as the one the Daybreak Café offered. Emily counted sixteen pages of choices, all accompanied by glossy color photos.

Dylan ordered the whiskey-glazed steak, baked potato and salad.

Emily ordered the grilled chicken, shrimp and steak trifecta, with spinach salad.

Both dinners were out within ten minutes. Both were absolutely delicious in the way that brand-spanking-new franchise food always was.

Xavier—who had been keeping a careful eye on them throughout—noted when they were done and promptly presented them with the dessert menu.

The Daybreak Café's sweets were all fresh and homemade. The selection here was clearly from the freezer section of a restaurant-supply store. The obligatory ice-cream sundae, New York style cheesecake and chocolate cake.

Emily breathed a small sigh of relief.

Until Xavier said, "Not on the menu are pecan pie, peach cobbler and hummingbird cake." He rested his forearm on the table and hunkered down, close enough to ask Emily impertinently, "So what do you say, Em? Ready to go out with me yet?"

EMILY RELEASED an exasperated sigh the moment she and Dylan left the restaurant and headed off down the sidewalk. "Okay, cowboy. You win."

He slung a companionable arm over her shoulders and leaned down to whisper in her ear, "I've never see you blush like that."

Emily let her head fall back to rest against the curve of his biceps. "That's because you and I weren't the only ones who heard what Xavier said." She tilted her head to one side and looked him in the eye. "Did you see the looks on the faces of those older folks behind us?"

Laughter rumbled from Dylan's chest. "Not to mention the high-school kids to our left."

Emily sighed. "His pass at me is going to be the talk of the town."

Dylan dropped his arm and took her hand instead. "Make that all of Laramie County. Although I have to say, you turned him down very gracefully."

They paused at the corner and waited for the streetlight to change. "I tried my best. Still, he did not look happy."

Dylan shrugged. "The kid's clearly not used to anyone telling him no. To anything."

A fact that could bode ill for the immediate future, Emily thought uneasily. Because guys like that, who were all ego to begin with, were usually a continuing source of trouble when scorned.

Dylan seemed to be thinking the same thing.

The light changed. They crossed the street, their fingers still loosely entwined. "Maybe we should pretend to be dating each other a little longer," Emily murmured.

Dylan guessed where this was going. "Give him time to find someone his own age?"

Emily relaxed in relief. "Right."

The matter settled, Dylan teased, "So back to our bet."

Emily heaved a sigh. "I guess I owe you a homecooked meal now, don't I?"

A comfortable silence filled the air as they walked across the park in the center of the green, past the covered picnic area, the community grills and the flower beds.

Furrowing his brow, Dylan finally said, "The only question is…where are you going to whip up that meal? My ranch or that apartment of yours with its nonexistent kitchen?"

Good question. Since both places had lots of privacy and close proximity to a bed.

Oblivious to the licentious direction of her thoughts, Dylan paused. "What exactly can you cook there?"

"Very little. And only in emergencies," Emily admitted candidly. "Say if I'm sick and I want to heat up a can of soup. Otherwise, I go down to the café and rustle up whatever I want there."

Dylan slowed his pace as they reached her building. Emily did, too. She was enjoying the stroll so much she did not want it to end.

"What do your dates think of that?" he asked curiously.

Emily made a face. "I don't cook for my dates."

Dylan lifted an eyebrow in surprise. "Then why did you offer to cook for me?"

Because that's what women do for the men they are interested in…. But not about to tell him how intrigued she was by him, Emily wrinkled her nose and pretended a detachment she couldn't begin to really feel. "Because it was a gamble, pure and simple," she explained, deadpan.

Dylan took her in his arms, bent her backward from the waist. "Like this?"

Emily knew he was daring her to protest. Aware anyone could see them standing on the street in front of her building, she grasped his shoulders for balance, and murmured, "Just like this."

Dylan lowered his head as if to deliver another slow, sultry kiss.

Emily's heart pounded—the suspense was killing her.

Rather than touch his lips to hers, Dylan looked deep into her eyes and murmured tenderly, "I thought we weren't going to do this."

Emily released a pent-up sigh. "We shouldn't…" she said wistfully. She turned her head ever so slightly in the direction from which they'd come. "Particularly with Xavier looking on."

Dylan blinked. "You're kidding me."

"Nope. He's standing outside the diner, staring in our direction, as we speak."

"Then just to make sure he gets the message, we'd better put on a real show."

Dylan half expected Emily to protest, given how she had only recently put on the brakes. Instead, she clutched him fiercely, gave her whole body over to the sexy embrace and kissed him with the vigor she had displayed from the very first.

And even though Dylan had sworn to stay emotionally detached, it suddenly dawned on him that she made him *want* to be involved. Not just physically and peripherally—as was his habit—but totally, with mind, body and soul. And no one knew better than him what a colossal mistake that would be, given their very different backgrounds.

Emily knew, from the moment Dylan set her back upright, that their tumultuous, just-for-show kiss was about to end. The only problem was, she didn't want it to end. Didn't want to stop feeling the coaxing sureness of his lips or the warmth of his body against hers. Didn't want to stop feeling that they really might have something special here, given half a chance. And she would have kept kissing him had the sheriff's car not pulled up right beside them and Deputy Rio Vasquez gotten out.

Rio took one look at them and shook his head. "I should have known." He grinned. "We got a call from the diner that a woman might be in trouble."

In unison, Dylan and Emily both pivoted. There, standing on the diner porch, in plain view was Xavier Shillingsworth. His attention still directed their way, he didn't bother disguising the wide smirk on his face.

"Obviously," Rio continued, shaking his head, "it was a prank…."

Dylan rolled his eyes. "Those crazy teens…"

Rio turned back to Dylan. "But as long as we have you here…" He paused, his expression serious. "The sheriff's department got word late today that your request to put your ranch on the community-service list was approved."

What? Emily thought in shock.

Rio shook Dylan's hand in congratulations, then finished cheerfully, "The district attorney's office notified us that your first juvenile will be coming Monday after school. It's Andrew Saunders, Simone Saunders's son."

Chapter Eight

Emily looked at Dylan, unable to contain her hurt. Maybe it was growing up "McCabe," but in her world friends and family shared the things that were important…and this definitely fell into that category.

"Why didn't you tell me?" she asked quietly.

Dylan's lips thinned. "I had a proposal," he told her curtly. "That didn't mean it would be approved by the court."

And clearly Dylan was not a man who counted on anything before it actually materialized.

Realizing once again how little information she knew about the lonesome cowboy, and how much she wanted to know, Emily touched his arm. She lifted her face to his and drew a breath. "It's a good thing—what you're doing."

He curled his lips derisively. "And that's a surprise because…?"

Open mouth, remove foot… When would she learn to speak with her head and not her heart, where Dylan was concerned?

"Obviously, you're a good guy," Emily sputtered on with as much reassurance as she could muster. "Anyone who works with damaged horses or mustangs has a good heart. No question."

Her attempts at damage control had only minimal success.

Dylan lifted a provoking eyebrow and waited a long moment. "I hear a 'but' in there…."

Okay, so he wasn't going to sugarcoat this or make it easy. Maybe she shouldn't, either. The heat of her rising temper warming her face, Emily shoved her hands in her pockets and rocked back on her heels. "You're not usually one to get involved in other people's problems."

He shrugged his broad shoulders. "That one landed on my ranch."

"So?" Emily reacted in kind, determined to confront him whether or not he wanted her to. "It doesn't mean it has to keep on being your problem, does it?"

Dylan looked her over in a manner meant to annoy her. "Andrew is curious about horses," he explained, as if addressing a particularly slow-witted student. "Ten to one, his mom can't afford for him to take riding lessons. Jobs on ranches usually go to those with some sort of experience."

Stepping closer, Emily let his condescending enunciation pass. "You're going to teach him to ride?"

Dylan shook his head. "I'm going to teach him that horses are to be respected and cared for, not terrorized and set free by a group of possibly well-meaning but ultimately destructive teenagers. He's got to *think* about the consequences of his actions before he acts."

Emily hesitated. "And you're going to teach him that?"

Dylan nodded. "Starting next week after school, when he shows up for his first work session."

"I DON'T KNOW about this," Simone admitted Monday afternoon, near closing. "I mean, I'm glad that Dylan presented the option to the district attorney and the sheriff's department, and that his ranch was quickly approved as a community-service site, but I'd almost rather Andrew be picking up trash on the side of the road. It seems a lot less dangerous than working with mustangs."

Emily measured yogurt, flour, water and malted milk into a mixing bowl. "First of all, Dylan is not going to put a greenhorn like Andrew in with Ginger, Salt and Pepper."

Simone watched Emily add the new sourdough to the original starter. "Maybe not deliberately, but what if Andrew doesn't listen well or follow directions and does something stupid and gets hurt anyway?"

Chances of that were slim, Emily knew, but for someone like Simone—who had no experience on a ranch—the danger of livestock combined with the great outdoors loomed large.

Emily paused to combine both doughs and cover them with plastic wrap. "Would you feel better if I were out there, at least during his first session with Dylan?"

Simone relaxed. "Would you mind?"

"Not at all," Emily said.

It was a beautiful spring day. Business at the café had once again been woefully slow—while the Cowtown Diner still had throngs of people standing in line to get in. Emily was hoping as soon as the newness of the establishment wore off, business for the Daybreak Café would pick up once again, but there was no guarantee of that.

It would be good to get away. And…she had promised to cook dinner for Dylan this evening as a payoff to the bet they had made. So the sooner she got out there, the better.

"Thanks, Emily." Simone hugged her in relief. "You're a real friend."

Andrew was less thrilled to have Emily give him a ride out to the ranch.

"Did Dylan tell you that you were going to need a long-sleeve shirt, jeans and work boots?" she asked. The teen was still dressed in the T-shirt, khakis and loafers he had worn to school that day.

"Yeah. They're in my backpack."

A lot of good they were doing there, Emily thought. She smiled. "Why don't you put them on now? It would be better to arrive at the ranch, dressed and ready to work."

"Whatever." Andrew grabbed his gear and headed, slow as molasses, for the men's room.

Emily glanced at her watch. Because Andrew had taken his sweet time getting over to the café from the high school, they had less than fifteen minutes to get out to the Last Chance Ranch.

"Are you going to be late?" Simone asked, worrying anew.

Emily looked at her friend. This was where being one of four kids who had given her parents their share of grief came in handy. She knew what her folks had done to regain control in any given situation. "Don't worry about it." She patted Simone on the shoulder. "Andrew's accountability starts now."

And, as Emily expected, Dylan held Andrew responsible from the get-go. "You're late," Dylan said.

"If Emily had driven faster…"

Not about to take the blame, Emily lifted a hand. "I was going the speed limit."

Dylan frowned. "I'm going to have to report that to the officer in charge of your community service, Andrew." He paused to let his words sink in. "He may extend it, as a consequence."

Andrew sulked. "By how much?"

Dylan shrugged, unsympathetic. "That will depend on the rest of the report I give. How cooperative you were, what the quality of your work is, how much you talk back to me and so on."

Andrew glared at Dylan but said nothing more.

Smart kid, Emily thought. Now if Andrew would just turn his whole attitude around….

Dylan handed Andrew a pair of work gloves and a shovel. "Grab that wheelbarrow and follow me." The two headed off to the stable. Emily stayed where she was, just outside the stable. As she expected, it didn't take long for the fireworks to start. The exchange that followed could be heard, clear as day. "That's horse manure!" Andrew bellowed in rage. "You expect me to shovel horse manure?"

Dylan's boots sounded on the concrete aisleway as he strode toward the door. "Once you muck out the stalls, you're going to clean them with a disinfectant solution and put down fresh hay."

More indignation followed from his young charge. "There are twenty stalls!"

"Then you better get busy." Dylan paused in the open doorway, his expression stern. "I'll be back in a few minutes to check your work."

And so it went, over the course of the next three hours. By the time Simone arrived at the ranch at six o'clock to pick Andrew up, her son was filthy, exhausted and even surlier than when he started.

"I'll see you Wednesday," Dylan said.

"I can't believe I have to do this for twelve more weeks!" Andrew muttered, stalking off.

Simone thanked Dylan and left with her son.

Emily turned to Dylan. She had spent the previous three hours gentling the two younger mustangs and was pleased that the same method they'd used on Ginger had worked on Salt and Pepper. "So what next?" she asked.

WHAT DYLAN WANTED to do was forget everything they'd previously agreed upon, take Emily upstairs into the shower with him and then to bed….

That plan was nixed by the vintage Corvette racing up his drive. Emily stared in the same direction as he. She looked shocked and displeased. "What's he doing here?"

Dylan grimaced and stared at the arrogant teen who was fast becoming a thorn in both their sides. "I'll find out."

Emily tensed. "You sure?"

"It's my property. I'll handle it." *And protect you from any more hassling in the process.* "In the meantime," Dylan said, handing her the soft cloth rope, "do you feel comfortable starting Ginger's training session by yourself?"

Emily looked longingly at the mustang. The idea of working with the horse obviously trumped whatever curiosity she had about Shillingsworth's presence.

"Absolutely. How do you want me to start?"

Briefly, Dylan explained.

Cloth lead coiled in her hand, Emily slipped into the round training pen with Ginger.

Dylan stayed just long enough to make sure the workout started off well, then turned and headed toward the adjacent parking area.

Xavier got out of his car.

Dylan strode toward him. "What can I do for you?"

"I want my shot at Emily, and I'm asking you to step aside."

If the nineteen-year-old wasn't so deadly serious in the request, Dylan would have burst into laughter. But it was clear as the seconds drew out that this was no laughing matter. This kid was used to getting everything he wanted, no matter what the cost. He obviously could not handle the fact Emily was not interested in him.

"I want her," Xavier repeated.

And that was the deciding factor?

"A cougar is the ultimate accessory for a nineteen year old mogul...is that it?"

Shillingsworth's ears reddened. "You laugh now, just like my dad, but I'm going to be rich and famous, and the success of the Cowtown Diner is just the beginning. By the time I'm thirty, I'll own hundreds of restaurants, all over the country, from all the different major chains."

Well, at least they knew the kid had a working ego—and then some. "Diversifying?" Dylan asked dryly.

Shillingsworth adopted a belligerent stance. "It's smart business strategy. And before you tell me I'm too young to succeed, consider the fact that many of the major companies today were helmed by college dropouts like Michael Dell, Bill Gates and Steve Jobs."

"I hardly think you're in their league, given the fact that your restaurant has only been open four days now."

Xavier smirked. "I'm glad to see you are counting. 'Cause I am serious about doing whatever I have to do to go out with Emily McCabe."

"Do yourself a favor and accept the fact that she's already taken, kid," Dylan said, realizing the words were truer than he wished.

Xavier chuckled. "Women like Emily never stay with guys like you. Sure, she'll dally with you for a while. You've got the whole mustang thing going for you, after all, and she clearly loves horses as much as she loves her café, but at the end of the day, she wants someone from a good family." Xavier snapped his fingers. "Oh, wait. You are from a good family. Or you *were*—until you got disowned. At birth, wasn't it?"

Shock rendered Dylan momentarily silent. "Who told you that?" he asked coolly.

Xavier regarded Dylan smugly. "My lawyer has a P.I. on retainer. It was not hard to uncover. The question is, does Emily know?"

No one in Laramie knew this, Dylan thought. Which was the way he wanted it. He stepped closer, telling Xavier with a

Get 2 Books FREE!

Harlequin® Books,
publisher of women's fiction,
presents

HARLEQUIN®

American ★ Romance®

GET 2 BOOKS

We'd like to send you two *Harlequin American Romance*® novels absolutely free! Accepting them puts you under no obligation to purchase any more books.

HOW TO GET YOUR
2 FREE BOOKS AND 2 FREE GIFTS

1. Return the reply card today, and we'll send you two *Harlequin American Romance* novels, absolutely free! We'll even pay the postage!

2. Accepting free books places you under no obligation to buy anything, ever. Whatever you decide, the free books and gifts are yours to keep, free!

3. We hope that after receiving your free books you'll want to remain a subscriber, but the choice is yours—to continue or cancel, any time at all!

EXTRA BONUS

You'll also get two free mystery gifts! (worth about $10)

FREE!

(H-AR-04/11)

look, if he pushed this harassment any further, Dylan would take the gloves off and give as good as he got. "What's your point?"

Xavier's glance turned to the round pen, where Emily could be seen working the mustang with long, gentle strokes of the cloth lead. "I'm sure Emily wants a man with a rich, powerful family, just like her own. She won't be happy, long term, without it."

Dylan's gut tightened at the possible truth to the words. "Get off my property."

"I'm richer...and more socially acceptable...than you will ever be," Xavier boasted. "So do us both a favor, cowboy, and give the lady to me."

GIVE THE LADY TO ME. What the hell was wrong with him, treating a woman like a piece of property that could be moved around at will? Dylan fumed, as Xavier got back in his vintage sports car and drove away much faster than necessary, leaving a cloud of dust in his wake.

Scowling, Dylan wheeled around and headed toward the round training pen. Emily had finished running Ginger and was now directing her in a counterclockwise motion.

He shut the gate behind him. Emily moved gradually toward him, still working Ginger until the two of them were close enough to talk quietly. "What was that about?"

Dylan shook off the query. "Nothing you need to be concerned about."

Indignation flared. "If it was about me, it's my concern."

Leave it to Emily to chide him because he was trying to protect her. "I thought that was my role in this scenario—as your man. To shield you from unpleasantness."

He watched as Emily turned her body to a forty-five-degree angle to the mustang. She relaxed her shoulders and dropped her gaze to the ground.

Ginger shifted toward Emily.

Emily moved away from the horse.

Ginger followed.

When Ginger nosed her shoulder and hair, Emily turned quietly. Smiling tenderly, she reached up to hold Ginger's bridle and stroked the white blaze down the center of the mare's face. The mustang luxuriated in the gentle affection as if she had been accustomed to it all her life, instead of just a few days.

Emily moved her hands over the horse's body, letting Ginger know she could trust her as much as Ginger already trusted Dylan. "So Xavier still hasn't given up on me?"

Dylan motioned Emily to return to the horse's face. He went to the wall and picked up a small featherlight training blanket. While Emily held Ginger steady, he placed the cloth on her back. "What do you think?"

Ginger bucked a little, trying to shake the blanket off.

Dylan calmed the mustang with a touch and a gentle word. He returned to get a light-weight training saddle, and brought it back. He set it atop the blanket and watched Ginger buck a little once more.

As Dylan expertly steadied the mustang, Emily said, "I think I'm going to have to speak to him."

He reached around and fastened the girths, so the saddle and blanket would stay on. Finished, he stepped back. He motioned for Emily to let go of the bridle. He took the cloth lead and began the process of driving the mustang around the pen, once again diverting her attention from the unfamiliar weight on her back.

Watching everything that was going on Emily kept pace with Dylan.

"I don't think that's a good idea," Dylan said as Ginger kept trying to buck the blanket and saddle off.

"Why not?" Being careful to stay clear of the powerful hind legs of the horse, Emily shot a glance at Dylan.

"That will only encourage him. He wants your attention—he doesn't care how he gets it."

"Then what do you suggest I do to discourage him?" Emily asked, exasperated. "He's seen us together on what at least looked like a date. He saw us kissing. He found me here, with you. Judging from what just happened, none of that matters. He still thinks he has a chance."

Dylan shrugged and stopped driving the mustang away. "We could get engaged." The reckless words were out before he could think.

Shocked, Emily turned toward him. "Be serious," she murmured clearly irritated that Dylan could suggest something so ludicrous. "We're not in love...not anywhere near it!"

Dylan stepped closer. "So marrying me is out?" he drawled, wondering if maybe Xavier Shillingsworth was right, if—in Emily's estimation—he wasn't in the McCabes' league for anything long-lasting.

"Definitely out," Emily said firmly.

DYLAN WAS JOKING, wasn't he? Emily thought. He hadn't really meant he wanted them to get engaged. Yes, they'd slept together, enjoyed each other's company and shared a love for horses, but beyond that they barely knew each other! So his suggestion couldn't have been for real. Perhaps it was some sort of test....

The question was why he'd want to appraise her that way.

Obviously, something had happened in his discussion with Xavier Shillingsworth. Something that he didn't want to talk to her about...

"You know my reputation with relationships...?" Dylan asked flatly.

Emily nodded. "That you're never going to be tamed by any woman…so no one would buy us becoming engaged." She forced herself to be logical. "Least of all my family. And trust me, we really don't want them stepping in at this point and getting involved."

Dylan studied her with a brooding expression. "Because they'd disapprove?"

"Probably," Emily was forced to admit. "Unless they thought we were right for each other."

Because we were in love.

She fell silent. "Not that I'm interested in giving up my freedom to get married, either," she said. "Besides, I doubt even that would discourage Xavier. He has such an overinflated image of himself." She paused. "I guess it's just going to take time and repeated rejection. Surely, he won't want to wait around for that long. I mean he strikes me as kind of an immediate-gratification type of guy."

He gave her a long look. "That's what worries me."

Emily waited.

"Sooner or later, Shillingsworth is going to figure out he's not going to get what he wants from you. When that happens, he's going to want you to pay for the rejection and he's going to lash out and try to hurt you in whatever way he can. And the place where you are the most vulnerable…"

With a start, Emily realized where Dylan was going with this. "…is the Daybreak Café," she finished for him.

Dylan nodded grimly.

Emily realized his assertion was true to a point. Her restaurant did matter to her immensely. But there was a place in her heart that was even more vulnerable—the place where her feelings for Dylan resided.

Chapter Nine

"About dinner," Dylan said, an hour later when the training was completed and all three mustangs were quartered in their paddock for the evening.

Emily tensed at the mention of their nondate. Her pretty forehead furrowing, she walked with him toward the house. "You still want me to cook for you this evening, don't you? As the loser for our bet?"

Dylan grinned enthusiastically. Maybe the two of them weren't meant to be lovers, but that didn't mean he didn't relish every second he spent with her.

Enjoying the disheveled state of her silky molasses hair, as well as how pretty she looked in her shirt and jeans, he asked, "Okay with you if I leave my truck parked right in front of your building all evening, instead of the alley behind?"

A pink flush flooded her sculpted cheeks as she stopped just short of his front porch. "You want everyone to see your pickup and figure out you're at my place," Emily deduced, not quite happily. "Including Xavier."

Especially Xavier, Dylan thought.

He sat down on the top step. Taking her hand, he tugged her down next to him. "Do you want to discourage him, or not?"

Emily heaved a disgruntled sigh and stretched her long shapely legs out in front of her. She wiggled her toes and examined the flower pattern on her red cowgirl boots. "I do."

Dylan planted a hand on either side of him and leaned back to stretch the kinks out of his body, too. Tilting his head toward Emily, he continued, "Then you have to make the kid understand in every way possible there is no chance for him to edge his way in."

Emily twisted her lips and studied Dylan with narrowed eyes. "This is a competition, isn't it?"

Actually, it was a hell of a lot more than that. Although how to explain…

Finally, Dylan shrugged. "For him it is, maybe."

"And for you?" she asked, nudging his thigh playfully with her knee.

Dylan ignored the heat the brief touch generated. With effort, he concentrated on the facts they could discuss. "As your pretend boyfriend, it's my job to protect you, Ms. McCabe."

She wrinkled her nose at the unexpected formality. "And that's all there is?" she pressed, searching his face. "There's no ego involved?"

Leave it to Emily to ask the really hard questions, Dylan thought moodily. "Of course there's ego involved." He felt compelled to be honest. "I'm a man, and you're allegedly with me. How would it look if I let that little know-it-all continue to make your life a lot harder than it has to be right now?"

Something shifted in Emily's eyes. Her teeth raked her lower lip even as her voice betrayed little emotion, "So this is all about your manhood."

It's all about protecting you, Dylan thought, but he wasn't sure how she would take that. "I don't want to see you hurt. I imagine none of your other friends or family do, either."

Again, something shifted. It was almost as if a force field went up.

"Okay." Emily rose abruptly and favored him with a brisk, efficient smile. "I'll see you at the café kitchen at eight o'clock."

"SOMETHING SURE SMELLS GOOD," Dylan said an hour later, when Emily met him at the front door of the café.

Emily sure looked good, too—although he had to wonder at her choice of a Daybreak Café T-shirt and a very worn pair of jeans. In contrast, he was dressed in his best shirt and pants.

Emily accepted the bottle of wine he'd brought with a smile, took his hand and guided him inside. "I'm glad you think so," she said in that excessively cheerful voice she used when welcoming patrons to her café.

She set the bottle on the counter and led him into the kitchen. There, already laid out on the stainless-steel prep table was a flatiron steak with jalapeño butter and a cheese enchilada on the side.

"I'm thinking of adding this to the lunch menu. What do you think?" Emily turned to face him, her attitude surprisingly professional.

The notion that this evening might turn out to be special swiftly faded.

Dylan chided himself for hoping otherwise. Of course a multitasking woman like Emily would put the task of cooking dinner for him to good use and use the experience to further enhance her business.

She gestured for him to sit down on the lone stool and then waited for him to taste.

Figuring he may as well, Dylan lifted a fork. In this, he was not disappointed. "It's delicious," he told her sincerely. "I think it would be a hit."

Emily set another plate in front of him. "What about the enchiladas?" She picked up her notebook and pen and began to scribble notes. "Were they hot enough? Too hot? Would you prefer a different kind of cheese in them, say Monterey Jack or jalapeño-Jack instead? Longhorn or mild cheddar cheese and onion filling is traditional, but queso blanco also adds something special." She sighed, thinking, then pushed several more plates at him for tasting. "But I don't know…I'm trying to appeal to the masses. And what about jicama slaw, instead of the traditional Southern?" Emily asked him rhetorically. "I tried that for a while, and to tell you the truth, it didn't go over all that great. The jicama has a taste that doesn't appeal to everyone."

"I think what you need here to advise you," Dylan said finally, when he could get a word in edgewise, "is a restaurant critic." He was only half joking. He knew what he liked. But everyone else…?

"Actually," Emily said, lighting up like a sparkler on the Fourth of July, "that idea's not half-bad, Dylan! Thanks!" She got up abruptly and went to the phone. While he watched, half in wonder, half in irritation, she made a call.

"Hi, Holden. You know that guy you were trying to get me to meet?" Emily motioned to Dylan to keep eating, then turned her back to him and began to pace. "Yeah, Fred Collier. Right. Do you think you could bring him by here tomorrow? Lunch is fine. And tell him, if possible, I'd like him to hang around for a short while after closing, so I can talk to him."

WELL, EMILY THOUGHT, after Dylan left a short time later, that was one way to end an evening on an unromantic note.

Make a "date" with someone else while your current guest is still on premises.

So what if it had been about business?

The point was she was honoring her debt to Dylan—by making him dinner—and honoring herself by keeping her options open.

And not letting this mano a mano stuff between Dylan and Xavier influence her one way or another.

So what if she got all warm and gooey inside when Dylan got protective of her in that distinctly man-woman way?

He'd said it himself. It was ego as much as friendship pushing him to become her white knight.

When Xavier backed off, as the teenager eventually would, and the business with her matchmaking family and the café finally settled down, she would no longer be a damsel in distress in Dylan Reeves's eyes.

She'd be a great gal he had once slept with, and that was that.

Much as she wanted to pretend it would turn into something more…the practical side of her knew the odds were against it.

So she had to protect her heart—and concentrate on the real problems in front of her.

Like saving her restaurant from going into a decline it might not recover from.

Because she knew better than anyone, once a café was considered second tier, for whatever reason, it often ended up faltering. Because it was just too hard to do the work if appreciative patrons did not show up in droves.

Hence, when Dylan came in for an early breakfast, she was too busy to come out of the kitchen to say hello. Ditto when Xavier showed up, a bunch of red roses in hand.

When the *Texas Traveler* magazine food reporter came in with Holden, however, she made sure the boyishly handsome "foodie" had everything he wanted. At the end of the lunch rush, she ushered him into the kitchen to see her work space and sample even more of the food.

"It's all wonderful," Fred Collier said, his kind green eyes shining with an admiration Emily found particularly gratifying.

Then he grimaced. "But I have to wonder where the crowds are. We've been here two hours, and the place has never been more than one-third full. While across the square, at the Cowtown Diner, the throngs have not abated in the least."

Emily's shoulders sagged. She had been hoping the restaurant critic wouldn't notice.

With typical gallantry, Holden explained, "It's the full-page ads and two-for-the-price-of-one meal coupons the franchise owner put out over the weekend in all the county newspapers."

Holden paused and looked at Emily.

Surprised by her shock, he shrugged inanely. "I thought you knew. I thought that was why you called. Shillingsworth is planning to extend the offer indefinitely. The coupons are reusable."

Emily's heart sank. "The diner will never turn a profit that way," she said, rubbing at the headache starting in her temples.

"Unless it's by sheer volume of customers." Fred Collier turned to glance out the window.

Sure enough, at two o'clock in the afternoon—usually a dead time for most restaurants—the Cowtown Diner was still busy as ever.

"Can you help her?" Holden asked his friend.

Fred smiled apologetically. "I'd love to, if and when your business picks up again. I only write about places that are standing room only, and right now, the Daybreak Café no longer qualifies."

"Thanks for coming by." Emily packed up some dessert for him and walked him out.

"Sorry about that," Holden said, when she returned.

Emily stared out the window at the competition that was

swiftly becoming a real thorn in her side. "Don't be," she told her big brother. "I needed a wake-up call. And this was definitely it."

"YOU'RE GETTING new outdoor chairs and umbrella tables now?" Dylan asked, later that same day.

The sound of Dylan's low, gravelly voice gave Emily a pleasurable jolt. Her heart had skipped several beats when he'd sauntered in for lunch half an hour ago but she'd been trying to ignore how ruggedly, casually handsome he'd looked in his soft faded denim shirt and jeans. It was bad enough she knew firsthand how his strong virile body felt pressed up against the naked length of hers without yearning to experience his hot, reckless brand of lovemaking again.

And now he was standing next to her once more, looking over her shoulder, studying what she had been studying.

"Yes. I am," Emily replied, and damned herself for sounding breathless.

She put the receipt aside and looked up the weather forecast on her computer. The rest of the day appeared warm and clear, but there was a fifty-percent chance of rain every day for the rest of the week. Which could sabotage her plans.

On the other hand, to do nothing was to automatically lose.

She turned back to Dylan. As long as they were still "friends" who helped each other out… "I have a favor to ask. Are you available tonight to help me drive to San Angelo to pick them up?" There were others she could ask to help her, but for reasons she chose not to examine too closely, she wanted him to go with her.

Speculation glimmered in Dylan's golden-brown eyes. "Sure," he said kindly. "Do you have a big enough vehicle?"

Trying not to feel too grateful he was in her life—for that

might mean starting to depend on him past the temporary time frame they'd agreed upon—Emily nodded. "I reserved a moving truck that will handle it all."

They set up an early departure time, and in half an hour, Dylan was at her door, ready to go. They took his pickup to the truck rental place and arranged to leave it in the lot there while they went to San Angelo.

Naturally, Dylan wanted to drive. A little overwhelmed by the sheer size of the truck, Emily had been hoping he would volunteer. She was independent, but not foolish enough to take on more than she could handle.

"So how did the lunch date with the food critic go?" Dylan asked casually, as soon as they were on the road to San Angelo.

"Fred Collier was a nice guy."

Dylan slanted her a glance she couldn't quite read. Too confident to be seriously threatened, he teased, "Good-looking?"

"Yes." Emily volleyed back, just as playfully. "Although I was more interested in what Fred might be able to do for my business."

Dylan sobered at the magnitude of the problems she was facing. "And...?"

Tension stiffened Emily's spine. "He's not going to write about the Daybreak Café, at least not right now." Briefly, she explained.

Dylan listened quietly, then shook his head in commiseration. "I'm sorry."

So am I. Emily settled more comfortably in her seat, shifting slightly to the left. Finding comfort in the intimacy swiftly springing up between them, she shrugged and forced herself to be as matter-of-fact as the situation required. "Holden's friend has a point. As did you, in a roundabout way." She studied Dylan's ruggedly handsome profile. His hair was rumpled and dark stubble rimmed the lower half of his face. He looked sexy and impatient. As impatient as she. "I have to be ready to compete a little more aggressively if I want the café to remain a viable business. And that means answering customer complaints a lot more responsively."

Hands competently circling the wheel, Dylan glanced at her curiously. The open collar on his shirt exposed the strong column of his throat. He had rolled up the sleeves of his shirt to just below the elbow.

Emily forced her gaze away from the sinewy strength in his arms, and told herself she was grateful for the seat between them.

She turned her attention back to business. "People have complained about the lines to get in since shortly after I opened two years ago. I don't have room for any more tables inside and to be honest, I liked the idea of having a sought-after commodity in such a small town." She laced her fingers together. "I thought the demand gave my place a sort of cachet not necessarily shared by some of the other larger restaurants in town."

Dylan murmured, "It was a small local haunt that anyone who was anyone knew about."

"And that alone made it special." Emily sighed. "But in retrospect I see that was a mistake."

Dylan listened, understanding that, too.

"And while I can't just put an addition on a historic building to increase seating in the café, I am permitted by the city to use the sidewalks surrounding the building. So I can put up tables that line the front and wrap around the corner immediately. And that's what I plan to do," she announced proudly, satisfied that she was back on the path to success. "Starting tomorrow morning, patrons will be able to dine alfresco."

Dylan knew that was what Emily hoped would happen. He couldn't help but wonder if she was just setting herself up for more disappointment.

IT WAS NEARLY ten-thirty that night by the time they returned to Laramie, precious cargo in tow. Eleven-thirty, by the time they unloaded the truck and set up the five umbrella tables and twenty chairs. And though Dylan had handled the trip well, he noted Emily was looking pretty tired as midnight neared. Which wasn't surprising, given she had been up since four that the morning. Whereas he, as usual, had slept in until six...

Her expression supremely content, Emily stepped back, looking at their handiwork beneath the glow of the street lights. "That's really nice, isn't it?" she asked Dylan.

He nodded in agreement. There was no doubt about it—the outdoor seating added a lot of charm to the storefront of her building. He wasn't sure, however, that a four-thousand-dollar expenditure was good for Emily *financially* at the moment. But since he had no idea what the café's bottom line was, he couldn't comment.

Instead, he focused on the positive. "The outdoor seating should help a lot, when the usual crowds return." He reached out to playfully tug the end of her ponytail. "I know I'll appreciate a shorter wait time for a table."

The corners of her soft lips turned up. "When," she repeated, her blue eyes sparkling. "I like the sound of that." She sighed, then added less certainly, "I only hope the prediction comes true as soon as possible."

Dylan consoled her with a hug. Forcing himself to keep it friendly, he gave her an extra squeeze and let her go. Stepping back from her, he held her gaze and reminded, "You're an amazing chef, Emily. Sooner or later, people are going to remember that and return in droves."

Emily's slender body tensed. She lifted her hands to her

head and removed the clasp holding her ponytail in place. "I hope so."

Dylan watched the spill of silky hair fall over her shoulders. Recalling their agreement, he tamped down his desire. "Want me to take the truck back to the lot?"

The tension left her shoulders. She slanted him a grateful glance, her weariness beginning to show. "If you wouldn't mind, that would be great," she told him softly. She looked around for the scissors she'd brought out of the café. "I'll stay and cut the tags off everything." She inclined her head slightly, added casually, "If you want to return, maybe we can have some pie à la mode or…something…"

Dylan didn't know what he was looking forward to more— eating one of the desserts she'd made or simply spending more time with her. "Sounds great," he said. Eager to get back, Dylan took off.

EMILY WAS NEARLY DONE cutting off the tags, when footsteps sounded. She looked up to see Xavier coming down the sidewalk, toward her.

Great. Just what she did not need!

Looking like a teenager who'd just had his car keys taken away, he started right in on her, demanding pugnaciously, "Why didn't you come out of the kitchen today when I brought you flowers?"

Emily wondered if the spoiled teen's bullying had ever worked on any woman. It sure did nothing for her. "I was busy."

His jaw thrust forward in what looked like a permanent pout. "You're making a mistake. You should date me, not Dylan Reeves," he told her scornfully.

Emily drew a bolstering breath and tried to be kind. "Xavier, I am sure there is a cougar somewhere right now who is calling your name. Some woman who would be delighted by the ardent attentions of a much younger man. It is just not me."

He blinked as if he couldn't believe the rejection. "I'm a great guy."

"Who is trying to run me out of business," Emily couldn't resist pointing out.

"A great guy who wants to succeed," Xavier insisted.

Emily moved to the next table and continued cutting off tags. "Then I wish you all the best. Now, if you don't mind, I have my own problems to deal with."

Once again, the kid refused to take the hint and, instead, followed her from place to place. "Dylan Reeves acts like a hero, but he's not." Xavier positioned himself so she had no choice but to look at him. "Dylan Reeves is a *criminal,* Emily."

Xavier's words carried an implicit threat that chilled Emily to the bone. She paused long enough to look him in the eye.

"What are you talking about?" she demanded evenly, all the while telling herself this could not be true.

He smiled smugly. "Dylan is a former juvenile delinquent, with a very long record. He spent time at the Libertyville Boys Ranch as a kid."

If that was correct, Emily thought, privately reeling at the news, it certainly explained a lot. Why Dylan had insisted on taking such a hard line with Andrew from the get-go. Why he was so involved with philanthropic work for the boys ranch. Maybe even why he was incredibly committed to his profession.

Determined to keep her feelings to herself, she regarded Xavier evenly. "Dylan Reeves is also my friend. And I don't let anyone talk trash about my friends."

Xavier glared at her. "You're a McCabe, a member of the most powerful, respected family in the state."

Was that why he had chosen Laramie as a site for his franchise diner? So he could hook up with her? The idea seemed bizarre and yet it made sense. The kid was definitely a social-climbing, billionaire wannabe who was looking for a shortcut to success. Perhaps he'd set his sights on the Laramie, Texas, McCabes, because they had powerful ties to ranching, oil and technology—as well as a host of other potentially lucrative professions, like commercial real estate development, movie-making and the designer clothing industry....

"There are plenty of other respected, powerful clans with single daughters. Girls," Emily emphasized bluntly, "more your age."

"None on par with the McCabes," Xavier argued back. "Or you."

Emily didn't really know what to say to that. It was true—her family was enormously successful. Enough to attract all kinds of people just looking for a quick ride to success. That didn't, however, make it right. She wished she knew a way to explain that entry into her world was not an immediate guarantee to personal happiness. But she knew that would fall on deaf ears to an obviously emotionally neglected kid like Xavier, who'd likely used money as the method to solve every problem. Deep down she sensed what the kid *really* needed was what she'd had—lots of familial love and attention....

Sometimes, too much attention.

"You'd really choose a small-time horse trainer over me?" he asked finally, aghast as the reality of the situation finally began to sink in.

"Horse whisperer," Emily corrected, "and I already have." She looked at Xavier with the little bit of patience and compassion she had left. "So I would appreciate it if you and I never had this discussion again, because it's clearly uncomfortable for both of us."

Hurt and astonishment gave way to boiling anger. "This is really the way it's going to be?"

"It really is," Emily stated firmly.

He balled his fists at his sides. "Then you're going to be sorry. You *both* will. *No one* disrespects me and gets away with it."

DYLAN ARRIVED, just as Shillingsworth stormed away. He parked his truck at the curb, in front of the restaurant, and came toward her. "What was that all about?" he demanded.

Emily's pulse picked up. "Let's take this inside, okay?"

Dylan searched her eyes, recognizing right away that something was wrong. "Did he hurt you? Because if he did…"

"He didn't touch me—it was just a verbal exchange." She led the way inside the café and shut the door after them.

Dylan waited, his brow furrowed in concern.

Emily swallowed hard and then drew a breath. "Xavier told me you had a criminal record."

Dylan's shoulders slumped. "It's true."

Hurt warred with confusion. "Why didn't you tell me any of this before—when it sort of came up because of Andrew?" she asked, feeling her cheeks heat.

He folded his arms. "It wasn't relevant to us."

She bore her eyes into his. "I thought we were friends."

His expression remained impassive. "We are."

Doubt reared. "Good friends tell each other stuff."

Silence fell as the moment of reckoning came. Emily expected Dylan to shut her out again, but he became unexpectedly gentle, let his guard down. "What do you want to know?"

Figuring if they did this right, it would take a while, Emily walked into the kitchen. "Everything. How and why you landed in juve—"

Dylan sat down on a stool. "I stole a car."

Emily set a chocolate-chip-pecan pie and a carton of vanilla ice cream on the prep table. "There has to be more to it than that."

His lips thinned. "There always is. There's no excuse for what I did."

Emily waited, but nothing else was immediately forthcoming. "What did your parents think?" she asked quietly.

"My father left before I was born. And my mom died during routine surgery when I was fourteen. This happened after."

"Did family take you in?"

"They were asked. But they didn't want me any more than they wanted my mom or me when she got pregnant at sixteen. So I was sent to foster care."

Emily's heart went out to him. "You must have been hurt."

Dylan inclined his head. "And angry enough to act out, the same way Andrew is acting out now. I fell in with a bad crowd. And did something really stupid, trying to prove I was tough." He paused, reflecting stoically, "Who knows what would have happened to me if I hadn't been sent to the Libertyville Boys Ranch? The people there turned my life around."

Emily cut two pieces of pie and topped them with ice cream. "Is that where you became interested in horses?"

Dylan accepted the plate and fork with a nod of thanks. "Learning to care for and about animals is a great lesson for kids, because animals are like us. They just want to be loved and understood."

He said that so easily. It was the first hint of real sentimentality she had seen in him. Emily yearned for more.

"*Do* you want to be loved?" Emily murmured curiously before she could stop herself. "Because sometimes, Dylan, I am not so sure."

Suddenly he grinned, as at ease with his sexuality as she was with being part of a family. He stood and walked around the table to take her in his arms. "In my way, yes, Emily, I want to be loved," he murmured softly.

An erotic thrill whispered through her, as hot and exciting as the feel of his body next to hers.

Emily tried to contain her disappointment that he wasn't more romantic in his view, that he still didn't want what she wanted—a love that would last forever. "You mean physically," she guessed, her pulse pounding.

Dylan shrugged, as matter-of-fact as ever. "It's a lot less complicated."

The question was, could she ever be satisfied with just that? *Was this a risk she was willing to take?*

Chapter Ten

Dylan didn't know what Emily was going to do. He knew what she was *tempted* to do. The slight hitch in her breath, the quickening of the pulse in her throat, the way she leaned slightly toward him, all told him that she was as ready to make love with him again as he was with her. At least, physically.

Emotionally was another matter. There, she still had her reservations, he decided. He couldn't blame her.

The two of them weren't well suited.

And never would be. Unless one of them changed significantly, and that was about as likely to happen as a snowfall in the Texas spring...

Her mood suddenly seeming as ambivalent as his, Emily edged away. "Well, I better go in. I have to get up at four, to get breakfast started in the café."

The gentlemanly thing to do would be to wish her well and let her go. But the desire flaring between them was almost impossible to resist. So Dylan found himself saying, "Are you planning on helping out with the mustangs tomorrow afternoon?"

Emily smiled. "Tell Ginger, Salt and Pepper I'll see them then."

Happy he had a reason to keep seeing Emily on a regular basis, Dylan promised he would.

Bypassing the temptation of a good-night kiss, for fear of

starting something that would be tough to step away from, Dylan headed home.

He spent the night dreaming about Emily, and woke, wanting her more than ever.

Storm clouds obscured the dawn.

By the time he had finished caring for the herd, rain was pouring down. Just in time to ruin Emily's breakfast rush. What was left of it, anyway.

Dylan drove by the café. Because of the weather, the exterior was deserted. Inside, the Daybreak Café looked just as sparsely attended.

While down the street, the Cowtown Diner had a respectable crowd inside, from the looks of it, and no line at all outside.

Knowing the hungry cowpokes had to be somewhere, Dylan headed for the feed store.

Inside, as he predicted, were three dozen cowboys and ranchers, using the inclement weather as reason enough to get their supplies in. Among them were all three of Emily's brothers.

Holden McCabe was the first to approach Dylan. He extended his hand. "I want to thank you for doing your part to help scare off Shillingsworth."

Not sure he should be accepting congratulations for having had a fling with Emily, Dylan returned the handshake, anyway. "I guess you heard—"

"About that arrogant kid setting his sights on Emily?" Hank McCabe prompted, joining them. "Everyone knows about it. Shillingsworth has been running all over town for a week now, embarrassing himself by telling people that Emily is going to be his cougar."

"Which in itself is no surprise," Jeb chuckled. "Given that our baby sis is such a bum magnet." He shook his head in mock consternation, then turned back to Dylan. "Fortunately, whatever she is pretending to have going on with you has caused the kid to change his mind. As of last night, Shillingsworth is saying he's no longer interested in Emily."

"Which of course is good news to us," Holden said.

Maybe not, Dylan thought, if the kid made good on his promise to seek revenge on their sister, and him.

Jeb ran a hand across his jaw, ruminating, "The mystery is that Shillingsworth ever thought he had a shot with her in the first place."

"Clearly, he doesn't understand what it takes to be a McCabe, or fraternize with one," another cowboy said, joining the group. "The sense of integrity and community…"

"Unfortunately," Holden said, "it doesn't matter how many suitable guys are attracted to her, or who we introduce her to, she always ends up with the completely unmarriageable types."

The feed-store owner walked up to join the group. "So maybe that means you have a shot," he ribbed Dylan with a grin. "Since you've vowed not only to never get married, but never be tamed by any woman."

Not about to publicly confess he was beginning to wonder if he should reconsider that declaration, Dylan shrugged.

Figuring Emily would not want anyone getting the idea that the two of them had once been intimate, Dylan kept up the expected ruse. "And for good reason, since freedom is the most important attribute a man can possess," he boasted with the expected machismo. "And the only thing that will ever guarantee happiness."

Everyone fell silent in an abrupt, uncomfortable way that let Dylan know he had missed something important. He turned slowly. Emily was standing in the open doorway of the feed store. The distressed look on her face said she had heard just about everything.

EMILY KNEW some guys acted as if matrimony was a prison sentence when they were standing around, shooting the breeze. It was one thing to be aware of that; another to witness it when she was the person supposedly carrying the potential ball and chain guaranteed to bring a lifetime of misery to whomever she one day married.

If she ever married.

That prospect seemed less likely every day.

In the meantime, she had a job to do. An awkward silence to end… "Hey, fellas," she grinned, sauntering nonchalantly forward, as if all her romantic hopes had not just been crushed to smithereens. She pulled the sheaf of coupons from the plastic protector in her hand and slapped them down on the feed-store counter.

"I hope you-all are hungry," she informed them in her sweet-as-pie Texas belle voice. "Because we've got quite the special going over at the café this morning. Buy one of our bottomless cups of coffee, and you'll get a free breakfast entrée. But the special is only good for today."

Hoots and hollers echoed throughout the warehouse-style feed store. There was a near stampede for the coupons and then the exit. Giving Dylan and her brothers no chance to say anything to her, she followed the hungry cowboys out the door.

As Emily had expected, the next few hours were incredibly busy. Although the tables outside were empty due to the downpour, the inside was hopping, just the way it used to be.

They served one hundred customers between seven and ten, and because she extended the special through lunchtime, another seventy-five after that.

Finally, it was time for closing.

And that was when Dylan Reeves walked in, his expression inscrutable. "I want to talk," he said.

"I can handle things down here," Simone said.

Bobbie Sue and Billy Ray concurred. "We'll clean up and close up," they said.

Figuring what she had to say to Dylan was best accomplished without an audience, Emily thanked them and led the way to her apartment over the restaurant.

Dylan shrugged out of his rain slicker.

He continued to look at her in his very sexy, very determined way. "About what you heard this morning at the feed store…"

"I think I got the gist of it."

He adopted a no-nonsense stance, legs braced apart, hands bracketing his waist. It would have been very intimidating had she allowed it to affect her. She didn't.

"The guys were just…"

Emily lifted her chin, daring him to try and spin it. "Having a chuckle at my expense? I know. Not to worry… I'm not serious about you, either, Dylan. I know better than that." And if she hadn't before, she did now.

"If I were interested in being tied down…" he said.

"Or tied up," Emily said, trying to lighten the mood with her flip comment. "I'm sure you'd just rush to the phone and call me."

Dylan ignored her comment and kept his eyes on hers. "You're an amazing woman," he told her quietly. "Everyone knows that."

How had this turned into the preliminary to a break-up speech? Emily wondered. And why did it hurt so much to think that was what it might be?

None of this had been real. She knew that. Didn't she…?

Years of being the kid sister, and hence the recipient of her older brothers' incessant teasing and interference, enabled her to regain her footing and pretend she was okay with all this.

Emily cleared her throat with exaggerated enthusiasm.

"And you're an amazing man," she recapped for him, cheerfully. "And neither of us are interested in marrying each other. So it's okay." She flashed a reassuring smile she could not even begin to feel. "Really."

The narrowed eyes indicated he disagreed with the attempt to just write off the mishap and move on.

Fearing that he would say something that would make her want to forget all about this and forgive him, she leaned closer still. "I get that we are just helping each other out in the short term." Emily took a bolstering breath and forced herself to hold his eyes in the same deliberate way he was holding hers. "I understand that you are a distraction for me from all my problems in the same way I am a source of free meals and an occasional horse wrangler for you."

Finally, he saw where this was going.

Dylan's lips thinned into a grim line. "You really think that's all we are to each other?" He studied her incredulously. "Aides-de-camp?"

She had to be logical, *stop* trying to turn guys into all they could be, *start* accepting them for who and what they were. And no matter how much it hurt, leave it at that.

Resolved that no matter what happened she would not cry, Emily faced Dylan. "That's a fancy term, cowboy, but given how all this started, with me asking you to be my pretend boyfriend? Glorified assistants slash occasional companions are all we can be to each other." She set her jaw and finished flatly, "All we should be."

That said, she showed him the door. The look on her face warned him not to expect anything to change any time soon.

Four days later, Dylan was in the Last Chance stable, commending Andrew on a job well done, when he heard the sound of Emily's car. He finished giving Andrew instructions on the making of the bran mash the horses would be getting for dinner, then walked out to the edge of the stable.

Emily was already heading toward the paddock where the three mustangs were waiting.

The younger two had already received their two training sessions for the day. Ginger was still waiting for her second schooling.

All looked glad to see the pretty dark-haired woman striding happily toward them.

Despite the way they had parted, Dylan was glad to see her, too.

"Why does being out on a ranch always make me feel better?" Emily asked the horses as she approached the pasture fence. The three mustangs, which had been standing together against the fence, moseyed over to greet her.

Emily stepped up on the second rail, the action making her tall enough to reach them. She smiled and ran her hands over the faces of the white filly and the black gelding, offering both a carrot for their trouble, and then turned to the leader of the mustangs, three-year-old Ginger.

The mare stuck her head over the fence, too, wanting her treat. Emily gave it to her first, then waited to see what Ginger would do.

Just as she'd done during the past three days of training Ginger pushed her head toward Emily, wanting to be petted.

Dylan knew how that felt, too.

Although they had seen each other numerous times over the past week, Emily had managed not to touch him once.

Or look him in the eye, either.

He'd given her the space she seemed to require, but that didn't mean he didn't miss her.

And that was a surprise.

Dylan had never missed any woman who had come in and gone out of his life. He'd never *allowed* himself to do so.

With Emily, it wasn't a choice.

He felt the way he felt.

Just as she felt the way she apparently felt.

"How is it," Emily continued in a soft voice Dylan would not have been able to make out, had he not been coming up behind her, "that horses in general and you in particular always lift my spirits no matter what else is going on?" she asked Ginger rhetorically.

Dylan wanted to know the answer to that, too.

Had he been a fool to think—even after the downward turn of their relationship—that Emily had rushed out to see him, as well as the mustangs? That she enjoyed his company as much as he enjoyed hers, even when she was still obviously angry with him? Or was he the one believing in fairy tales now? Indulging in wishful thinking…hoping someone would change even when they showed no real disposition to do so…?

As if sensing the conflicted nature of his thoughts, Ginger nickered softly in response and swung her head toward Dylan, dipping her nose.

As Dylan reached up to pet the mustang, Emily turned slightly and caught sight of him. He inhaled the familiar scent of her hair and skin. "You look tired." The words were out before he could stop himself.

She lifted an eyebrow at the unusual display of over-protectiveness.

Dylan had to admit he was a little stunned himself. He didn't usually comment on the shadows beneath anyone else's eyes. Even eyes as pretty as Emily's.

The intimacy in her expression faded as quickly as it had appeared. "It's been crazy busy at the café all week, from open to close," Emily said with a shrug. "Even with the tables outside, we are jam-packed."

Dylan was glad she was getting her clientele back.

It was easy to see why.

Thus far this week, the specials had changed every day. After the success of her free entrée with a cup of coffee, she had gone on to offer a half-price breakfast special—which had been a fruit plate, biscuits and breakfast casserole. The third day it had been all the blueberry pancakes you could eat, for a dollar. This morning, there had been huge fifty-cent cinnamon rolls and coffee. Dylan had eaten there all four days.

The lunch specials the café was showcasing were just as amazing.

"I guess the additional promotions and the specials are really working out for you?"

Emily beamed. "I've got all my regular clientele back and then some."

"Good to hear." He liked to see her so blissfully happy and content.

Emily released a stress-filled breath. "Which is why I need to be out here today. Breathing in the fresh air and spending some time with the horses really helps me unwind."

"You could do that at your folks' ranch."

Emily moaned and playfully clapped both hands over her ears. "Yes, but at a price. My parents would want to talk about the financial details of my café."

Dylan had wondered about that himself—even though he knew it was none of his concern.

But as long as they were on the subject... "They might have a point."

Emily lifted her hand. "I know I'm losing money, Dylan. I had no choice. Xavier was driving me out of business with his coupon deals."

Dylan's muscles tensed. "How is Shillingsworth?"

"I don't know—I haven't seen him. He put some college kid in charge of the Cowtown Diner and went back to the city a few days ago."

This was news.

Dylan searched her face. "You think he's given up?"

Emily bit her lip. "I wish. But…probably not. He's probably just figuring out some other way to exact revenge on me."

"Let's hope not."

Whatever the situation was, Emily did not want to discuss it. "Enough chitchat. What are we going to do with Ginger today? Put the riding dummy back on her back and lead her around the ring?"

With Emily's help, Dylan had gotten the smart, adventurous horse used to the blanket and saddle. Then he'd progressed to the noisy plastic bags tied to the saddle horn. They flapped against her sides, where an actual rider's legs would go. And finally, a riding dummy that weighed fifteen pounds, strapped to the saddle. Now, she was ready for more. As was the woman beside her.

"Actually, I had something more exciting in mind. That is if you're up for it," Dylan said.

THIS WOULD BE a whole lot easier if she weren't still so attracted to the lonesome cowboy, Emily thought as Dylan stepped into the paddock.

Throat dry, she watched him attach a lead to Ginger's halter and lead the mustang back through the fenced aisleway to the round training pen.

As they walked together, he explained, "It's time for Ginger to get used to the weight of a rider. She likes and trusts you, so I'd like that rider to be you."

Excitement bubbled up inside her, along with pride at having been chosen to do this. "I won't get thrown?"

Dylan favored her with a sexy half smile. He took the

blanket and saddle and put them on the big mustang. "Not if we do it my way," he said reassuringly.

While Emily gently stroked Ginger's forehead, Dylan bent to attach the girths around the mare's middle.

"And how is that?" Emily asked, gazing into the horse's dark eyes. Ginger stared back at Emily, her ears fixed forward, in a sign of happy curiosity and trust.

"I'll show you." Dylan secured the stirrups and walked around to take the mare by the bridle. He stood close to Ginger's head, on the left. Then gestured for Emily to come around, on his right.

"I want you to put your left foot in my right hand, instead of the stirrup. Take hold of the saddle horn and lift yourself up, so you are leaning against the middle of the saddle. Stay as erect as you can, to give her a chance to get used to your weight. But you can still jump off and back, away from her, if need be."

Ready for action, Emily nodded her understanding.

Dylan gave her waist a reassuring squeeze. "I'm going to hold on to your left leg with my right hand, to keep you steady at the same time I'm holding on to her with my left hand. Okay?"

Emily had seen Dylan do the same thing with the riding dummy, so this was merely a reenactment of what they had done the previous day. Only now she would be the rider.

She looked at Ginger, doing her best to imbue the mustang with confidence and courage, then turned to Dylan. "Let's do it."

The first time she hoisted herself, Ginger promptly moved in a way that shifted Emily right back off.

Dylan caught Emily in one arm, holding on to the now-prancing Ginger with the strength and gentleness of his other.

"It'll happen," he told them both softly. "You just have to trust that it will."

Emily nodded. Took a breath. And tried again.

And again she was shaken back off.

And so it went.

For the next dozen or so times, Dylan was right there to catch and steady them both.

Eventually, it became a game.

Ginger chewed her bit and pushed them both away with her nose, dancing back and forth all the while.

Emily knew then that Ginger never would be a docile, mutely accepting pet. After all, this was a mustang who was meant to state her opinion often. As if on cue, Ginger turned her head from side to side and whinnied softly, her voice carrying throughout the training pen.

"We're going to get through this," Emily told her, already imagining the day she'd be able to take Ginger on a wild canter through the surrounding plains and meadows. Horse and rider as one…. And then, almost as suddenly, as if she were imagining it, too, Ginger allowed Emily to grab the saddle horn, step up and hold on.

THE TWO FEMALES WERE a beautiful sight, Dylan thought in satisfaction as he let go of horse and half rider and used the long cloth lead to urge them both to circle the training pen.

By now, Emily had one foot in the stirrup. Her body was resting against the saddle, her middle draped across.

Ginger was moving forward, not quite trotting, not quite walking.

Testing, it seemed.

Liking what she felt.

Of being one with the equally feisty and daring spirit that was Emily.

And just that suddenly, Emily did what they had *not* agreed upon, Dylan noted furiously. She shifted and brought herself all the way down into the saddle.

Caught as much by surprise as he, Ginger reared up on her hind legs.

Emily slid backward.

Momentarily lost her balance.

And somehow managed to hang on before all hell broke loose.

Fear roiled through Dylan as he watched Emily being catapulted off, falling into the wooden-railed side and finally landing with a hard thud on the dirt floor of the round training pen.

Chapter Eleven

Dylan didn't know whether to read Emily the riot act or kiss her. The truth was he wanted to do a little of both. Ginger was equally on edge; the mare had backed up against the wall of the round pen and was standing still, head hanging down slightly, ears up and motionless.

Dylan swiftly closed the distance between them and dropped down beside Emily, who was now up on her elbows, looking more peeved than in pain.

He watched her sit up farther and test her limbs, apparently finding nothing broken. His relief morphed into anger. "You could have been seriously hurt."

Emily accepted his hand and struggled to her feet. She dusted off the seat of her pants and tilted her head. "But I wasn't."

Dylan kept one eye on Ginger, who was still standing against the wall, watching them both. Figuring the best thing to do was put the horse to pasture, he went back to Ginger and took her by the lead. "If I'd had to tell your parents you'd been injured…"

Emily came toward them both. "No point in worrying about something that never happened." She boldly met his eyes. "I'd like to keep going."

Wishing he didn't want to pull Emily into his arms so badly, Dylan said, "You really want to get back up on that horse?"

Emily removed the elastic band from her hair. "Halfway. No more," she declared smoothing the dark strands away from her face, putting her hair back into a ponytail. "Just to let Ginger know nothing's changed, that this is still going to be expected of her."

Dylan studied the flush in her pretty cheeks and the furrow of determination formed along the bridge of her nose. "You promise you'll do what I ask *and no more* this time?"

Emily took a step closer and said softly, "I promise."

So up she went.

This time, maybe because she felt she had made her point in tossing Emily to the ground, Ginger accepted the rider's weight against her side.

And this time, Dylan did not let go of either of them.

Half an hour later, they finished the training session on good terms. Emily praised Ginger warmly as she turned her out into the paddock and then faced him.

In that instant, Dylan noted the stain on the back of Emily's burgundy cotton shirt. It was right across her shoulders, beneath the caked-on paddock dirt, and he knew exactly what had caused it.

"Now you are really overreacting," Emily said, minutes later, after he had said goodbye to Andrew and escorted Emily into the ranch house.

Dylan did not think so. He tapped her in the vicinity of the spot. "Unless I miss my guess, that's dried blood."

Emily didn't look all that surprised.

Which meant that she knew she'd been scraped up at the time. She just hadn't wanted to stop what she was doing to tend to the skin injury.

His exasperation with her grew.

Emily shrugged. "So I'll go home and take care of it."

Feeling the pressure building at the front of his jeans, Dylan decided to dial it back a notch. He had to stop wondering if she missed touching him as much as he missed touching her. He had to stop thinking about kissing her again. Concentrate on the here and now, and the first aid obviously required.

He eyed her injury, knowing it bore further inspection. Sooner rather than later. Enough time had elapsed already, given the bacteria-laden setting. "How?" he countered. "There's no way you can reach that on your own."

Emily looked up at him. "You're offering to bandage me up?"

"Yes." Figuring enough time had been wasted, Dylan motioned for her to turn around.

Emily made a face but obliged.

Dylan plucked the collar of her shirt away from the nape of her neck and peered down. Best he could tell, the scrape was four-by-six inches or so. Smack-dab between the shoulder blades. "I'll take care of it for you," he offered dutifully, "but it's going to have to be thoroughly cleaned first, and the best way to do that is to hop in the shower."

Wincing, Emily adjusted her shirt. "You really are a pain."

He regarded her with barely masked impatience. "I could always call your family, let one of them take care of it." Then he wouldn't have to go through the torture of touching her without making love to her.

Emily continued to scowl at Dylan. "Don't you dare." She sighed loudly and gave him a vaguely accusing look. "And don't you dare tell them I got thrown, either. My parents would have a fit."

And maybe with good reason, Dylan thought, given the poor judgment Emily had shown earlier today.

Hand beneath her elbow, Dylan steered Emily toward the stairs. "I'll need the duffel bag in the trunk of my car…."

He remembered the extension of her closet. No one could

ever say Emily did not come prepared. "Give me your keys and I'll get it for you."

Emily dug in her pocket for her keys. "Thanks."

Dylan tore his gaze from the enticing flatness of her abdomen. He did not need to be thinking about the snug fit of her jeans any more than he needed to be thinking about the clinging cotton of her shirt. "Towels are in the linen closet. Bathroom's—"

"I remember where it is, cowboy." Emily slapped the key in the palm of his hand, her fingers warm and silky against his skin.

Because, Dylan thought, she had been there before. Not just upstairs, but in the same place he'd like to have her now—*in his bed.*

He searched for some nonexistent gallantry and shot her a glance. "I'll get you some clean clothes." *And while I'm at it,* he promised vehemently, *I'll do my best to obliterate these reckless thoughts before they land us both in hot water.*

DYLAN WAS AS GOOD as his word, Emily noted. By the time she had washed the dirt off her face, he was back, her duffel bag in hand.

Unfortunately, the only things in there were another pair of jeans and two pairs of socks.

He lounged on the other side of the open bathroom door. "Problem?"

Yes, Emily thought in frustration, there were no extra undies. But Dylan didn't need to know that, she told herself sternly. Pleasantly, she explained the portion of her predicament she wanted him to know about. "Apparently, all the extra riding I've been doing, coupled with my lack of time to get any laundry done, has left me without a clean shirt."

"Want to borrow one of mine?"

Emily tried not to think what it would feel like to be

wrapped in his clothing. And not want to make love with him again. "If it's okay."

He nodded, as overtly casual as she. "No problem."

By the time Emily got out of the shower, a clean navy blue shirt was hanging on the inside of the bathroom door. He had managed to put the shirt there without opening the door more than an inch or actually coming in. Truth be told, Emily was a little disappointed about that.

She'd wanted to think she was so irresistible that a rogue like Dylan couldn't help but make a pass at her.

Instead, he was nowhere to be found.

Sighing her disappointment, while simultaneously applauding his good sense, Emily finished toweling off. Despite the warm soak, the scrape on her back was still raw and stinging. She debated over putting on the bra and panties she had just taken off, but they were as sweaty as the rest of her discarded clothing, and she couldn't bring herself to put them on again when she felt so nice and clean.

Frowning, she slipped on Dylan's shirt, rolled up the sleeves and buttoned all but the top closure. The soft navy cotton fabric voluminously cloaked her middle and floated down past her hips. Grimacing, she tugged her jeans on over her bare skin. Luckily, they were one of her oldest, softest pairs.

Telling herself that her lack of undies didn't matter—it wasn't as if he hadn't seen her naked before, anyway—she put on her socks, bundled her filthy clothing together and headed down the stairs.

Dylan was in the kitchen, standing next to the counter, as he went through the items in the Last Chance Ranch first-aid kit. He turned, devilry gleaming in his eyes. "It's not too late," he drawled.

Yes, Emily thought wistfully, as her heart skipped a beat, it was.

It was way too late.

He winked as the corners of his lips turned up into a warm, teasing smile. "If you want to call a real medic…"

Emily rolled her eyes and set her bundled clothing on the floor. Working to still her racing pulse, she stepped toward him. He was right. Taking a light, carefree attitude was best. "Don't be silly. You can do this."

The look on his face said he knew that—he just didn't know if he should. Emily understood his hesitation. After the feed-store debacle, they'd agreed not to make love again, yet already the tension between them was sky-high. And she hadn't even partially disrobed yet.

Telling herself she could handle this, just the same way she handled him, Emily turned. Her back to him, she unbuttoned the second, third, fourth closures. Easing the fabric open, she simultaneously clutched it to her breasts and pushed it back and down so the shirt fell across her shoulders and lowered over her spine.

She winced as cool air assaulted the raw scrape that traversed the skin between her shoulder blades.

"You're lucky you didn't break anything." Dylan picked up a spray mix of antiseptic and anesthetic lotion.

Emily closed her eyes in anticipation of more pain, muttering, "I'm too stubborn to break anything."

"I hear that's what your father used to say when he was rodeoing," Dylan murmured.

She exhaled. "I guess a little recklessness runs in the family," she agreed.

"No doubt." His warm breath brushed over her skin.

Emily hitched in a breath as the liquid hit her scrape, stinging at first, then promptly cooling into blissful numbness.

Relieved, she let out another slow breath.

Looking into his eyes at that moment would have been dangerous, but she could feel Dylan's smile. It was as warm and soothing as his touch.

"Now for the antibiotic cream," he said.

Emily tensed despite herself. "That's got to hurt less, right?"

"You shouldn't feel much at all," Dylan predicted.

He was right. She felt no pain with the application of the thick white cream, but there was no way *not* to feel the gentle strokes of his fingers across her back. No way not to be aware of the pearling of her nipples beneath the shirt he'd lent her, and the curl of desire sweeping through her insides.

By the time he had finished, it was all she could do not to tremble, she wanted him so much.

Sounding a lot more unaffected than she felt, he closed the cap on the tube. "We could bandage this, if you want."

"I think it's probably better to leave it open to air, don't you think?"

Emily tried to adjust her shirt with her free hand, but found that to be an impossible task.

Again, Dylan stepped in to help, lifting the fabric away, easing it up and over her shoulders with gentlemanly care.

Embarrassed by her unprecedented vulnerability, glad for the modest coverage, Emily pushed the buttons through the holes. Only when she was sufficiently cloaked did she turn back to face him once again.

Aware her whole body was still aching with the need to be touched and loved, Emily forced herself to put aside her yearning and look Dylan square in the eye. "Thank you," she managed.

Dylan rested a companionable hand on her shoulder. "You're welcome." He paused, smiling. "Thank *you* for helping out with Ginger."

"But not for taking too much upon ourselves, too fast?" Emily teased, wishing he would throw caution to the wind, forget their earlier promises and kiss her.

Dylan shook his head, in deadpan censure, then he dropped

his hand to his side. "Had you not done that, you never would have been thrown," he reminded mildly.

Emily sighed. She guessed it wasn't going to happen. He wasn't going to make a move on her after all. And really, she schooled herself firmly, it was for the best.

She stepped back. "I'm aware of that." Unable to bear the intimacy in his eyes, coupled with the need welling inside her, Emily looked down at her clothing. "Unfortunately, I can't go back into town dressed like this." She screwed up her face comically. "Not without causing a lot of talk anyway."

He tapped her playfully on the nose. "And we certainly don't want that."

Emily wanted Dylan to pull her against him and kiss her, taking the decision out of her hands.

"You can use the washer and dryer, if you want." He stepped back. "I'll make myself scarce and give you your privacy."

Here it was, Emily thought, the opportunity to put the fierce yearning aside and keep to their agreement. And maybe she would have had he not seemed tempted, too. The daredevil inside her was back, stronger than ever.

She curled her hands over his biceps. "That's not what I want."

Dylan swallowed. "If I stay, you know what is likely to happen."

"And you think that'd be wrong for me?"

His eyes gleamed. He came closer, all lazy, swaggering male. "You're a McCabe. You're meant to be married to someone from a family just like yours."

And marriage, Emily knew, was not what Dylan wanted. He might have, of course, if he'd believed in happily-ever-afters. But he didn't.

And that meant she had a choice to make too that would require her to take a giant leap of faith.

She splayed her hands across Dylan's chest, her determination to succeed stronger than ever. "I know what everyone thinks. That I have to have what my family wants for me. That I can't be with any man without trying to change him, but that's just not true," she whispered, her growing feelings for him giving her courage. "I can be with you—without asking you to change—just like you won't ask me to change." She wound her arms about his neck and rose on tiptoe. "Let me prove it to you."

Dylan's jaw set. "I'm not the kind of guy you need, Emily. I never will be."

Emily ignored his quelling expression and instead focused on the pulse racing in his throat. "What I need is my freedom, Dylan," she stated stubbornly. "Just like you need yours."

Dylan's eyes shuttered to half-mast. Already, he was giving in. "Emily…"

Luxuriating in his surrender, she pressed a finger to his lips. "No promises, Dylan. No thinking about what tomorrow will bring. Just…this." She kissed him, sweetly, tenderly.

"You say that now," he protested against her mouth on a rough exhalation of breath.

Emily took both his hands in hers. "And I mean it." She stared deep into his eyes, promising, "We'll be together as long as it feels right, as long as I need a boyfriend to stave off Xavier and run interference between me and my family, and you need help with the mustangs." Her heart pounding, she drew a bolstering breath. "After that, we'll go back to each doing our own thing and go our separate ways. With no complications and no regrets. Just a few memories to keep us warm on cold winter nights."

Dylan studied her, still gripping her hands. "You're talking friends with benefits?"

Emily shrugged, unwilling to put even that much of a restriction on what it was they were agreeing to. Aware he was hard and male and strong in all the ways she had ever wanted, she whispered back, "Friends with *temporary* benefits, Dylan."

Looking as if she were everything he had ever wanted, too, Dylan smiled. He threaded his hands through her hair and brought her face up to his. Slowly, he lowered his lips, tilted his head to better accommodate the kiss. His eyes closed. "You drive a hard bargain, cowgirl. But one I feel compelled to accept." He kissed one corner of her lips, then the other.

"What can I say?" she whispered fiercely, pausing to deepen the kiss. "I want what I want…and what I want, Dylan, is you."

So much…

"Well, then," he answered in a deep, sexy voice that kindled her senses all the more, "let's make it happen." He reached for the zipper on her jeans. As he drew it down, cool air assaulted her skin. The warmth of his palm followed, then his touch. She surged and writhed, surrendering her body, and then he was pressing her back against the counter, pushing her pants all the way off.

"Dylan," she moaned, her legs opening even wider. His hand slid between them, stroking the tender insides from knee to pelvis and back again. She was teetering on the edge… bursting with heat and sensation. "Dylan," she cried out, even more urgently.

His eyes dark with passion, he slid downward. Smiling at what he found, he teased her gently, "I like you without panties." And then before she could do so much as take a breath, his mouth was there, his fingers parting the delicate skin and sliding inside. Driving her crazy. Making her shake as more moisture flowed, until she quivered in ecstasy and nearly collapsed with the pleasure of it. Swells of almost unbearable sensation sweeping through her, she opened her eyes. "I wanted to wait for you."

"You will," he promised hoarsely. Rising, he opened her

shirt, claimed the softness of her breasts. Admiration shimmering in his eyes, he stroked her nipples. Then he captured her skin in a kiss so hot and sweet and tender it had her shuddering all over even as she demanded more.

Not to be undone, she unbuttoned his shirt and pressed forward so her nipples rubbed against the work-honed muscles of his chest. The delicious friction made her groan. That, along with her subsequent kisses, made him hard. Really hard. So hard he did not protest when she finally tore her lips from his, eased down the zipper of his jeans and dispensed with his clothes from the waist down.

She was determined to make this as good for him as he had for her. She tempted…discovered…adored, until his legs were taut and his breath was rasping in his chest. He brought her upward, to sit up on the counter. He stepped between her legs with a resolve that had her surrendering all over again.

Together, as erotic moments passed, they looked their fill.

"I don't know how we got so lucky," Dylan rasped out, "but for once I'm not going to question it." And then he was kissing her again, shifting his strong hard body until it became part of hers, and she was lifting her hips and wrapping her legs around his waist, bringing him closer still.

Caught up in something too powerful and primal to fight, Emily took him into the warmth of her body, and then discovered their bodies were made for each other after all. Awash in sensation, she let sheer abandon overtake her. Their ragged breaths meshed as soulfully and completely as their hot, passionate kisses. And then it happened, just as he'd promised it would. He pressed into her as deeply as he could go and they were soaring, flying free. Boundaries dissolved in a wild, wanton pleasure unlike anything she had ever known.

Afterward, they clung together, breathing hard. And Emily

told herself it was a very good thing she was *not* in love with Dylan or he with her. Because if that had been the case, they'd *both* be in a heap of trouble.

MORNING CAME far too soon, and with it a whole new host of problems. "Xavier Shillingsworth is back," Bobbie Sue Everett reported, shortly after the café opened.

Telling herself that nothing was going to alleviate the glow she felt, Emily continued whisking eggs. "How do you know that?"

Bobbie Sue frowned. "Because he just took the corner booth and ordered one of everything on the menu, to be brought to him one dish at a time."

Emily sighed. "Or in other words, he intends to be here awhile."

"All morning, from the way he was talking."

Dylan—who'd been occupying a seat at the counter—ambled into the kitchen. Seeing him reminded Emily of the hot, passionate lovemaking of the night before and the fact that she could not ever recall being this happy or feeling this adored.

Dylan took up a proprietary post next to Emily, all lazy, swaggering male. "Want me to get rid of Shillingsworth?" he asked.

Emily shook her head. "He has as much right to be here as any other customer, and if he wants to pay me several hundred dollars for the privilege, so be it."

Dylan came closer and gently touched her cheek. "You know he just wants to make trouble."

Emily's heart warmed, still she cautioned, "You don't need to protect me."

Dylan grinned. "As you pointed out to me in the past, needing and wanting something are two different things. And since I am your, uh…"

"Pretend boyfriend?" Simone put in, from the other end of the griddle.

Emily blinked at the unexpected sarcasm.

"Hey." Simone held up a hand in her own defense. "I know I owe you a debt of gratitude for everything you've done for my son, Dylan. Since Andrew started doing community service at Last Chance Ranch, he really is turning around, attitudewise. But that doesn't mean I want to see Emily hurt. And games that get this complicated usually end up hurting someone."

"Well, it's not going to be either of us," Emily told her friend firmly, exasperated to find yet another person trying to watch out for her. She looked the tall handsome cowboy in the eye. "Dylan and I know where we stand."

The question was…would friends with temporary benefits be enough to make either of them happy, even for the short haul?

Fortunately, Emily had little time to think about it, as the café began to fill with cowboys looking for the day's bargain. Dylan went back to sit at the counter and keep an eye out for Shillingsworth. Emily and Simone manned the griddle and ovens, while Bobby Sue and Billy Ray Everett waited tables.

All would have gone smoothly, had it not been for the astonished scream, which reverberated through the Daybreak Café, a short time later.

Emily dropped what she was doing and rushed into the dining room. A female diner Emily had never seen before was standing, still screeching, and pointing at her plate. Aware that every head had turned toward the female diner, Emily raced forward. "What is it?"

"A cockroach!" the woman shrieked even louder. She pointed at her plate. "Right there!"

Sure enough, Emily noted in disgust, there was a dead three-inch cockroach, peeking out from beneath a half-eaten

Western omelet that Emily had prepared herself. Horrified, she grabbed the plate. "I am so sorry."

"How could this have happened?" The woman threw down her napkin and bolted for the door, as if the hounds of hell were after her.

And so it went.

At seven-thirty, another patron Emily had never seen before found a shard of broken glass in his bowl of oatmeal.

At eight-fifteen, a young man in a college T-shirt discovered what looked like a mouse tail inside a breakfast tortilla.

Through it all, Xavier sat in his booth, a fake look of concern on his face.

By then, Emily's brothers had all come in to the café. They were standing with Dylan, near the cash register.

"Normally, I'm against physical solutions to problems...." Holden said.

Jeb squared his hat on his head. "But some pranks just aren't funny."

Hank nodded grimly. "And a person needs to be shown the door."

"I agree." Dylan looked all three of Emily's brothers in the eye.

When had Dylan lost his outsider status and become one of them? Emily wondered in shock.

"Well, I don't." She forced herself to keep a low profile. "I object to the kid garnering even that much attention." She cast a look over her shoulder at the smugly observing teen. "Don't you guys get it? He wants to be the center of attention. He wants to be able to lodge a complaint that I refused to serve him."

"You have every right to do so," Jeb said.

"And if I do, he'll make a fuss and try to figure out a way to get it in the news. This isn't the kind of publicity that I want.

Trust me, guys. Just ignore him and he'll eventually give up, pay his bill and leave."

All four men disagreed.

But for some reason Emily couldn't decipher, her three brothers looked to Dylan to decide. "It's whatever Emily wants," Dylan said finally.

Emily had very little time to regret her decision.

Because just then, the door opened, and an inspector from the health department walked in.

"ARE YOU OKAY?"

Emily looked at Dylan, glad he had remained with her during the day's upheaval, yet uncertain how to answer that. She shut the blinds and put the Closed sign on the door. Turning back to Dylan, she ran a hand through her hair. "Considering the Daybreak Café just got an eighty-three out of a possible one hundred points?" Renewed horror ran through her. "Dylan, I've never gotten less than a ninety-eight!"

Dylan followed her into the kitchen. "The inspector knows those incidents this morning were bogus."

It hadn't made a difference, though, Emily thought glumly. "He still had to come out and do his job. And give me demerits for the customer complaints, even though he couldn't find a single thing that would have substantiated the validity of the infractions." Feeling weary to her soul, Emily sat down on a stainless-steel kitchen prep stool. She buried her face in her hands.

Dylan rested a compassionate hand on her shoulder. "If it's any consolation, your brothers and I still want to take Shillingsworth out behind the barn."

Emily rolled her eyes. "McCabes don't do violence on others and you know it. It doesn't matter what the situation is, there is always a civil way to resolve it."

His expression serious, Dylan pulled up a stool and faced her. "And a not so civil way," he said bluntly.

Emily smiled. "You certainly inspired uncivil notions in me last night," she murmured, the feel of his knee pressed against hers, reminding her of the unbridled pleasure they had discovered.

His eyes crinkled at the corners. "Same here...but we digress."

Emily had never had a boyfriend so willing to take on her problems. "So we do."

"It seems to me I heard tales of your dad dueling in the streets with that movie star Beauregard Chamberlain over your mother."

"That was years ago, and he just did that to get my mother's attention. It's why she married my dad. Or so the legend goes."

Their eyes locked, held. A feeling of peace stole over her.

"I could challenge him...."

Emily caught the humor in his glance. "I don't think so."

"So what next?" Dylan asked eventually.

Emily traced the shape of his hand. "What do I want to happen? Or what do I think will happen?"

He caught her palm in his. "The latter."

Emily relaxed into the comforting warmth of his grip. "I imagine my parents—" she winced as the sound of voices could be heard outside the back door "—will have gotten the news and be stopping by."

Seconds later, Shane and Greta walked into the café kitchen, just as Emily had figured. Behind them was an entire contingent of McCabes. Brothers, sister-in-laws, aunts, uncles, cousins. Everyone, it seemed, who had been in the vicinity and was remotely available had joined the force.

Emily's aunt Claire, a noted lawyer, stepped forward. "You

may not be able to sue yet, but you can certainly send a formal cease-and-desist letter…."

Kevin McCabe, from the sheriff's department, advised, "I say we start an investigation."

And that, Emily found, was just the beginning of the free-flowing support from her family and friends. Everyone had an idea. Everyone was willing to help.

Everyone except, it turned out, the person she most wanted at her side.

Chapter Twelve

Several hours later, Emily found Dylan right where she expected him to be—on his ranch. For once though, he was laboring indoors. "Why did you leave?" she asked quietly, her emotions in turmoil as he ushered her inside his ranch office.

Looking handsome as could be in a blue chambray work shirt and jeans, he sat behind his oversize oak desk and squinted at the computer screen. "It was a McCabe family caucus. I'm not a McCabe."

Emily edged closer, her heartbeat accelerating as she took in the familiar fragrance of sandalwood and spice. "You were welcome to stay."

"I thought it was better, under the circumstances, if I didn't."

Emily knew her family in its entirety could be overwhelming. They seemed that way to her sometimes. However, she still wanted Dylan to be a part of her life. And her extended relatives were a huge part of that.

He pushed Print and, rocking back in his chair, watched the invoices appear in the tray. "What did you come up with?"

Emily leaned against the corner of his desk. She liked the intimacy of being here with him like this. "My uncle is starting an investigation into who the customers actually were... where they came from. Apparently, after they made the calls to the health department—which were from disposable cell phones—the accusers vanished into thin air."

Dylan reached past her for a stack of preaddressed envelopes bearing the Last Chance Ranch logo. "Which makes you think they were part of the scam?"

Emily studied the movements of his large, capable hands, wondering how he could be so strong and yet so tender, too. "Beau thinks they may have been professional actors. He's using his connections to check with the talent agencies and theater troupes around the state." She watched Dylan match the invoices to envelopes. "Hopefully, they'll find something soon. Unfortunately, Xavier has already tried to get it in the local news."

He shifted his gaze to her face. "Any takers?"

"Not so far." Emily twisted her lips in consternation. "Everyone smells a setup."

Dylan added stamps. "As do I," he said with a frown.

Restless, she stood and shoved her hands in the back pockets of her jeans. "All my regular customers are pretty enraged. The phone has been ringing off the hook."

Dylan dropped the envelopes in the out basket. He switched off his computer and stood. "Is that why you came out here? To get away?"

And be with you.

But not sure how that revelation would go over, Emily swallowed.

"And help train the mustangs," she said, wary of driving Dylan away with her sudden neediness. Because that was new, too. This wanting to be with a man more than anything else in the world.

She pushed on, "I know my family can be overwhelming at times…especially when they're all together…."

His expression became inscrutable. "I told you before, I don't do family drama," he said.

Emily remembered but that explanation gave her only partial relief. Maybe because she was starting to want so much more.

But that hadn't been their agreement she reminded herself. Their agreement had been to be together as long as it was good, without trying to change each other. To live and let live…the way each had become accustomed to doing.

"Right. Anyway…" Emily moved closer. "We now know what Xavier meant when he said he was going to make me pay. The question is…" She paused to give her words weight. "What is he going to try and do to you?"

Dylan shrugged. "Nothing much he can do. Financially, I'm in good shape. And I doubt anything he would have to say about my horse-whispering abilities would hold up under scrutiny."

Emily relaxed. "True. All potential customers would have to do is look at the mustangs, and how far they have come in just ten days, to know how talented you are."

Dylan reached past her to turn off the desk lamp. "I also have a lot of current and former clients who will vouch for me."

The near contact sent a thrill shimmering through her. Emily dropped her hands and stepped back. "I still think he's going to try and hurt you, the way he hurt me today."

"And I think we shouldn't worry about it. Not tonight, anyway." Dylan slid a hand beneath her elbow and steered her out the door, toward the paddock where the mustangs were quartered. He grinned. "Not when your three pals are waiting to see you."

To Emily's delight, they spent the next few hours working with all three horses. Dylan still would not let Emily get all the way up in the saddle with Ginger—he wanted the horse to get used to Emily's presence at her side first. So they worked out, this time in complete accordance with Dylan's wishes.

Then they fed and watered the mustangs, before heading to the ranch house.

"You staying for dinner?" Dylan asked Emily casually as they crossed the threshold.

Her heartbeat accelerated. "You inviting me?" She worked to keep her voice casual.

Dylan nodded, matter-of-fact. "We could go out. My treat this time."

Emily groaned at the thought. "Please don't make me go back to town, not tonight. I don't want to run into anyone who wants to talk about the sabotage, and I sure as heck don't want to look at the Cowtown Diner from my apartment."

"Then here on the ranch, it is. Got anything to change into?"

Emily had made sure to replenish the "wardrobe" in the trunk of her car. Glad things had returned to normal between them, she winked and picked up the pace. "Several things, as a matter of fact."

An hour later, both of them had showered and changed into fresh clothes. Dylan stood at the stove, searing, in a cast-iron skillet, two rib eye steaks he'd pulled from the freezer.

Realizing this was how "friends with benefits" operated, Emily found a package of mixed veggies to steam in the microwave, and a crusty loaf of bread. Cold bottles of beer and hunks of white cheddar completed the menu.

"That looks delicious," she said, as the two of them set their meal on his kitchen table.

Dylan got out the steak sauce. "I'm good at everything I do. Or hadn't you noticed?"

Emily added napkins. "Modest, too."

"Hey." He made no effort to stifle a cheeky grin. "It ain't braggin' if you've done it."

Emily gave him an amused once-over. "Spoken like a true Texan," she drawled right back.

His gaze roved her V-necked T and jeans, before returning to her face and hair. "You look good in here." His gaze lingered on her lips.

Emily tingled in every place his eyes had touched, and some places they hadn't. "Right at home, hmm?"

He held out her chair. "Like you belong." He paused, hand on the top rung, then added, more specifically, "On a ranch—not in an apartment in town."

Emily's hopes lifted and fell in short order. Again, she shook it off. So Dylan hadn't said what she'd initially thought he had meant. So what? He was still paying her a compliment.

She patted his arm amiably in return. "Those steaks look good." She turned away. "Let's eat."

Dylan caught her by the waist and brought her back against him. While her pulse raced, he gently nipped her ear, lifted the veil of her hair and kissed her throat. "And after that," he whispered sexily, "I've got plans for us, too...."

DYLAN WAS AS GOOD as his word.

Unfortunately, the bedside alarm went off at three-thirty.

Emily groaned as it continued to blare in her ears. Normally, she didn't mind getting up and going to the café. Cooking in the early morning to an appreciative crowd was one of her very favorite things.

But then, she thought, stretching languidly, most days she hadn't been up most of the night making love. Most nights she hadn't fallen asleep wrapped in Dylan's warm, strong arms.

He reached over and shut off the sound of country radio. With a moan that echoed her own reluctance, he nuzzled her hair affectionately. "Tell me you heard that."

Emily groaned again. "I heard it." Her voice was muffled against the satiny skin of his shoulder.

He chuckled, kissing her again. "Tell me you're getting up."

Emily opened her eyes and slowly sat up. "Against my will…I am." She reached over to take his hand. "Thanks for a great night," she said softly, knowing she had never felt so appreciated and well loved.

He kissed her knuckles tenderly. "Ditto."

They looked at each other in companionable silence.

Emily had no idea what was on his mind, but there were many things on hers, none of which were permissible to say under their current arrangement.

Things like…*I know what we agreed upon but I might be falling in love with you, anyway.*

Or…*I wish I never had to leave, that we never had to be apart again.*

And even…*How would you feel if we changed the rules… just a little bit?*

But Emily couldn't say any of that because she was a McCabe and she had given her word that her fling with Dylan was casual and temporary. And like it or not, she had to honor that commitment as surely as she would have honored any other that she made.

So she reached over and turned on the bedside lamp.

Through sheer force of will, she tossed back the covers— and saw Dylan's gaze drift hotly over everything that wasn't covered by eyelet lace camisole and tap pants, as well as everything that was.

Emily felt a flashpoint of desire that resonated deep within her heart. "If I don't get up now," she told him, resisting the magnetic pull between them, "we both know what will happen." The same thing that had happened last night…and the time before that…

Regret that she was leaving glimmered briefly in his eyes. Fortunately for them both, he too was a realist.

Dylan threw back his covers and got up. "You're absolutely right about that," he agreed gruffly.

For once in her life, Emily found herself wishing she weren't quite so independent and strong willed. She headed for her clothes, tossing the casual words over her shoulder. "So…I'm out of here as soon as I'm dressed."

Dylan was right behind her. He clamped a possessive hand on her shoulder. "I'll go to town with you."

That was a surprise, since the diner wouldn't be open for several more hours. Emily turned, curious. "Assigning yourself my protector?"

Dylan shrugged. "Something like that." He paused. "Do you mind?"

Emily shook her head. "Not at all."

FOR EMILY AND DYLAN, the next few days were blissfully calm and happy. The two of them worked with the mustangs every afternoon, ate dinner together each night and then made love. Dylan drove into town with Emily in the mornings and had breakfast with her before heading back to the ranch to work.

Their only worry was another onslaught from their teenage nemesis. Fortunately, the "McCabe posse" was having some success linking the incidents in the café to Emily's competitor, and they hoped to soon have enough proof to be able to simultaneously pursue legal action and clear her name with the health department authorities.

"Well, I for one, am glad to see Shillingsworth get what he had coming to him today," Simone said Thursday afternoon, when the Daybreak Café had finally closed and all that was left was the cleanup.

Bobbie Sue and Billy Ray brought in filled bins of dirty dishes and silverware and began loading them into the big commercial dishwasher. "The Cowtown Diner didn't have a single customer today, except for a few tourists who wandered in at midday," Bobbie Sue said.

Billy Ray added, "And it's been that way for the last three days."

Andrew walked in from school, backpack slung over his shoulder. "Shillingsworth has started laying off staff. Half my friends who got jobs there got let go yesterday, due to lack of business."

The past couple of weeks had been so tumultuous, in so many ways. Emily didn't want to take anything for granted. She grimaced. "It could still pick up."

Everyone else exchanged looks. "I don't think so," they all said finally, in unison.

"People have wised up," Simone declared. "It doesn't matter how young or inexperienced or even rich he is. They know who and what he is. They're not going to support his kind of tactics."

"Yeah," Andrew said, helping himself to a leftover piece of pie and a glass of milk. "There are too many good guys around here, like Dylan, for anyone to put up with someone that cutthroat and mean-spirited."

Emily breathed a sigh of relief. "I just wish it hadn't happened." The uneven business had wreaked havoc with her books.

Which was why she had finally allowed Jeb to bring his friend over to meet her.

DYLAN HAD JUST FINISHED paying the farrier when Xavier walked into the stable.

"Falling down on the job, aren't you, cowboy?" Shillingsworth began.

Not sure whether to feel sorry for him or just loathe him completely, Dylan took a firm grip on the kid's arm and propelled him away from the quartered mustangs, who had just had their feet trimmed and their first set of shoes put on.

Left to the wild, and their own devices, they would not

have needed protection on their tender feet, since wild horses moved from place to place only when necessary. But now that they were becoming domesticated, the horses would be expected to cover greater distances, often on hard ground. Hence, protecting their hooves was essential.

Dylan continued pushing Shillingsworth out the door. "I'm sure you have better things to do with your time than visit me."

"You're right about that." The kid regarded him with derision. "But I didn't want to let the opportunity go by to clue you in on your lady friend."

"This isn't high school," Dylan announced flatly.

"Meaning what?" Xavier taunted. "Because you and Emily are over twenty, you both have an open relationship? Because if that's the case it would certainly explain why she's sitting in the café, getting cozy with that guy her brother took over to meet her a little while ago."

Another fix-up engineered by Emily's brothers? Dylan knew there were supposed to have been three. Only two had happened thus far. Still, he would have expected Emily to refuse the opportunity, now that he and she were so involved.

"Thanks for your concern," Dylan told Shillingsworth drily, calmly escorting him all the way to his Corvette. "But Emily and I have an understanding."

The restaurateur's snide expression remained unaltered. "That covers her cheating on you?"

Dylan opened the door with his free hand and shoved the spoiled teen behind the wheel.

It wasn't cheating... It probably wasn't anything. There was no reason for him to feel this jealous and threatened. "Goodbye, Xavier."

He sneered. "I'm still going to get even with you, you know."

Dylan knew the kid would *try*. In reality, there was very

little he could do. He leaned over and offered parting advice with as much kindness as he could muster. "One day soon you're going to figure out this is not the way to win friends and influence people in Laramie, Texas."

"And one of these days, you're going to have to leave this all behind and go back where you came from, too!" Shillingsworth scoffed.

He started the engine and spun the car around. Deliberately driving over the lawn around the ranch house, he roared off in a plume of dust.

Telling himself he had nothing to worry about, Dylan went back to work. He expected Emily to show up the same time Andrew did, around three-thirty. Instead, Simone dropped her son off.

As had been the case all this week, Andrew showed up dressed in rugged Western clothing, ready to work. "What do you want me to do first, boss?" He squared his hat on his head. Anticipating the usual answer, he looked around for the wheelbarrow and shovel.

Dylan lifted a staying hand. "I've already mucked out the stalls."

Andrew raised his brow in surprise. And for good reason, Dylan noted, since that was usually his first job of the day. "It's time you learned how to lead and saddle a horse," he explained.

Excitement shone in Andrew's eyes. "Ginger?"

Not quite. "You can learn on my horse, Hercules. For now, Emily is the only one besides me who can help with Ginger."

Andrew grinned and followed Dylan into the stable with all the excited swagger of a kid heading to his first rodeo. "Miss Emily is really good with the mustangs, isn't she?"

Dylan nodded. Funny, how much he enjoyed working with this kid. He had never figured he would be a mentor. But there was no doubt about it—he was making strides with the once-recalcitrant kid. "You're right about that." He smiled. "Emily's got the McCabe gift with horses."

"Speaking of Miss Emily... She tried to get you on the phone but you didn't answer, so she asked me to tell you she would be pretty late getting here today. She's talking with this friend of her brother's."

So what Shillingsworth had said was true. Dylan handed Andrew the bridle and bit, and asked casually, "At the café?"

"They started there," Andrew confirmed, "but then went up to her apartment 'cause they needed privacy. Anyway, she'll be here later. When she's done with whatever she and the other guy are doing."

"Thanks for the info." Dylan picked up the blanket and saddle. He continued down to Hercules's berth, sure the meeting was innocent enough. It was the fact it was happening at all that bothered him. Had Shillingsworth been right? Did he have cause to worry?

Chapter Thirteen

Emily walked into the stable and stopped in her tracks. Dylan was standing next to the mustang, a dandy brush in hand. "You're grooming Ginger?" This was a first as far as she knew.

"About to." Dylan flashed her a look that was all business. "Want to help?"

"Sure," she said with a shrug, checking her need to greet Dylan with a long, heartstopping kiss. His body language and curt tone made it painfully clear that he was not in the mood for romance.

Her glance averted, Emily entered the stall and rubbed the mustang's face and neck. "Hello, pretty girl," she murmured softly. "Did you miss me? I missed you today."

Dylan took the left side of the horse. "I think this is happiest I've seen Ginger look all day."

Blissfully aware how content she felt whenever they were together, too, Emily plucked a rubber currycomb from the bucket of tools. "Surely you exaggerate," she said dryly. "I know Ginger adores you."

"And how do you figure that?" Dylan lifted his brow.

"Because you're good in the saddle, too." Abruptly aware of the double entendre, Emily blushed. "Er, corral. Okay…" She kept on combing and gave him a humorous glance that begged for mercy. "I'm going to stop now."

Because none of this is coming out right. And because, although I can't quite say why, I have the feeling something is a little off between us, unlike the last time we were together.

Adding to her worry, Dylan looked disconcerted, too.

Like he wasn't sure what to make of the shifts in their relationship, either. First they were strangers, then adversaries who'd joined forces to ward off her matchmaking parents—and an unwelcome suitor—and now finally temporary lovers who'd agreed they weren't destined to be anything serious.

"I get what you mean," he resumed his usual easy-going manner. "And you're correct. Horses respond to trainers who are in control of their emotions."

And Dylan was that, all right, Emily thought ruefully to herself. The only time he let go of his emotional armor at all was when they were in bed.

Once they were out of each other's arms, it was business as usual. A friendship based on a shared love of horses and ranch life and good, Texas-style food.

But even that was not guaranteed to last, she knew.

Dylan had been clear on that. And she had concurred.

Deep down, she wished she had never made the pact with Dylan to keep things casual. But she was leery of changing anything and have the lonesome cowboy end up feeling trapped.

So she would do as promised and make it easy on him when the time came… She just hoped that wasn't for a good long while. Years, even…

Using short, straight strokes, they brushed the mud from Ginger's coat. Dylan seemed as lost in thought as she.

"You're awfully quiet," Emily said eventually, wishing he would confide in her more. Instead, she felt like there was still so much she did not know. Might never know if it were left up to him.

Dylan rubbed a damp sponge over Ginger's face. "It's been a long day."

Emily stood on the other side of the horse and finished working the knots out of Ginger's mane. She moved so she could see Dylan's face. His expression was as maddeningly reserved as ever. Finally, she guessed, "Are you ticked off at me for not making the training session this afternoon?"

"No." Dylan used a massage pad over the mare's sleek neck muscles. "I understand you had other stuff to do."

Emily worked on the knots in the tail. "I did." She fell silent once again, thinking.

"Now who's exceptionally quiet?" Dylan teased. He gathered up the tools, gave Ginger a final pat and stepped out.

Realizing they had probably done enough for the first session, Emily praised Ginger softly and stepped out of the stall, too. She joined Dylan in the cement-floored aisle and fell into step beside him. "Sorry. I was thinking about my meeting with Randall Schwartz, the guy who sells prepared foods to restaurants. He's a friend of Jeb's."

Dylan led the way into the tack room. He deposited the tools on a shelf bearing Ginger's name. In a corner, there was a sink. "I thought you weren't interested in that." He gestured for her to go first.

Emily pumped soap onto her hands. "I wasn't… I'm not." The aroma of juniper and mint filled the air. She lathered, rinsed and shook off the excess moisture.

Dylan stepped in for his turn. His shoulder nudged hers slightly in the process. He turned, his face close to hers. "But?"

Emily couldn't help but note how strong and large his hands were. She swallowed, pushing away the memory of his gentle, capable touch. "I'm beginning to think I may have to consider cutting a few corners."

They walked out of the stable.

Realizing she needed a sounding board, and she wanted it to be Dylan, Emily continued matter-of-factly, "My business is in trouble."

Dylan escorted her across the yard. "Because of the competition?"

Emily nodded and sat down on one of the rough-hewn chairs on his porch. "I went over my books this afternoon, after closing. Because of everything that has happened the last few weeks…" she sighed, recalling, "First—no customers. Add to that, the financial loss I took on all those specials I offered to draw patrons back in."

Misery engulfed her as she shook her head. "This month is so far in the red that it's wiped out my entire profit for the year to date." She swallowed, loath to admit, "I'm going to have to dip into my personal savings to make payroll and pay the suppliers next week."

To Emily's relief, Dylan did not judge her fiscal recklessness. "Which is where Randall Schwartz comes in."

She nodded. "Randall showed me how I could cut costs if I used wholesale pre-made biscuits, muffins and desserts instead of making them up fresh every day. He has a full line of precooked meats, veggies and casseroles, too."

"But…?"

"We're back to my original problem. I don't want to sacrifice quality. At all. Ever. 'Going microwave' guarantees the demise of any restaurant. Proof of that is in any of the many once-popular chains that went bellyup, or are still around but are definitely third or fourth tier now."

Dylan lounged against the porch railing, listening, his hands braced on either side of him.

In the background was a spectacular April sunset, the blue sky framed by a horizon streaked with shades of pink, red and gold. "Well, then, you don't want to do that," he said, understandingly.

"I absolutely do not want to do that." Emily vaulted to her feet again, too restless to stay in one place for long. She paced back and forth, the sound of her boot heels echoing on the wood-plank surface. Whirling around, she threw up her arms in frustration. "The whole point of coming to the café is to get hot, home-cooked food when you're too tired or busy to prepare it yourself."

Dylan settled more patiently on his perch and sent her an admiring glance. "That concept has worked well for you so far."

Emily trod closer. "The tough thing is, I'm going to have to keep offering some sort of daily special if I want to keep the customers coming in the door."

Dylan's eyes narrowed. "You've spoiled them?" he guessed.

Emily rubbed the tense muscles at the base of her neck. "You know how it is. Everybody loves a bargain...."

Dylan motioned for her to turn around and he took up the kneading for her.

She closed her eyes and let herself relax into his soothing touch. Eyes still closed luxuriantly, she let out a long breath. "And I get that it will bring people in the door." She pressed her lips together in stubborn determination. "Which is something I need to keep doing, whether the Cowtown Diner survives the recent downturn in their business or not."

Needing to look into Dylan's eyes again, Emily swung around. She placed her hands flat on his chest before pulling away once again. "The question is, how do I afford to do it?" she mused.

The subtle lift of an eyebrow. "No answers?"

Emily grimaced in frustration. "Not a one. Not tonight anyway!" Restless again, she began to pace.

After a moment, Dylan left his perch and sauntered slowly toward her. He looked as if he wanted to distract her with a kiss. "I'm sure you will work it out," he soothed.

Emily's heart began to race. "I'm sure I will, too, in time."

Not sure she could do this tonight, have a no-strings-romp in Dylan's bed without falling head over heels in love with him—and wanting a lot more than a temporary fling out of the bargain—Emily forced herself to ease away.

Ignoring the flash of disappointment on his face, Emily kept the focus on her business difficulties. "Certainly there a lot of people chomping at the bit to help me."

"Like your parents."

"And my brothers, and their friends." She hesitated. "Remember Aaron Markham, the accountant slash tax lawyer I met a couple weeks ago?"

Dylan nodded, his eyes guarded.

"Well, he's called several times, wanting to meet with me again. He's sure he can help. Even Fred Collier, the food writer has called me back, wanting to know if 'anything has changed' that would give him reason to come back to the café again, anytime soon…."

Dylan's glance narrowed. "Sounds like he wants a date."

Was Dylan jealous at the thought of her spending time with another guy—someone who had the seal of approval from her brothers and was in the market for marriage? Or was Dylan just as perceptive as ever?

Emily shrugged, her uncertainty increasing. "Maybe. I didn't really get that vibe from Fred the day we met, but sometimes, after the fact, you begin to think…hey, maybe I should have gone after that or pursued someone a little more aggressively."

Or eschewed immediate pleasure and held out for more than just a temporary fling…

But she hadn't.

And Emily couldn't really say she regretted having made

love with Dylan, even if she was not going to get a forever commitment out of him…

Because to have not ever felt what she'd felt in his arms would have been a lot sadder than having to one day say goodbye.

Or that was what she kept telling herself.

She snapped out of her reverie when she realized Dylan was giving her a really odd look.

As if he had figured out at least part of what she was thinking. The part of her that wanted to throw a lasso around him and put a wedding band on his finger.

Emily struggled to contain the self-conscious warmth moving into her face. She really had to get a grip. "You know what I mean."

Dylan nodded. Determination tightened every strong, tall part of him, and he inched closer. "I know you're a fine looking woman," he murmured, wrapping his arms around her waist.

Emily caught her breath as the softness of her body slammed into the hardness of his. She splayed her hands across his chest, felt the beat of his heart. "And you're a fine looking man. But it takes more than looks to make a match, Dylan."

"I agree." His low voice rumbled in her ear. "It takes this." He bent his head to hers. The kiss was electric and all-enveloping. Her body responded like tinder to a flame, and she kissed him with growing passion. Knowing she was caught up in something too powerful to fight, shivers of unbearable sensation swept through her.

"And this," Emily told him. She pressed into him, her breasts lodged against the solid warmth of his chest, her tummy cradling the hardness of his sex. She kissed him back, again and again, melting against him in complete surrender.

Ready to take the pleasure where and when she could, she let her own desires…for marriage, for family…go.

Maybe they didn't want the same things out of life, Emily reasoned. Maybe they never would. But they still had the here and now. And heaven knew, a love affair this passionate was not likely to occur again. Not in her lifetime.

Dylan threaded his hands through her hair. "I want to go upstairs and make love to you all night long," he whispered. Tilting her face up to his, he captured her lips in one long, sweet and tender kiss.

It was the kind of kiss that made her feel loved. That made her feel wanted. That made her feel she was already his, and vice versa.

A thrill soared through Emily.

His hands shifted down her spine, fitting her against him. His lips found the soft, sensitive spot behind her ear. He drew back to look into her eyes. "Tell me you want the same thing."

Another shiver went through her.

Emily laced both hands around his powerful shoulders. She steadied herself even as her lips, still damp from his kisses, curved upward. "That sounds like a proposition I can handle."

"It's more than a proposition." Dylan bent, laced an arm behind her knees and swung her up into his arms. Holding her tightly to his chest, he carried her inside. His eyes danced with an affectionate light. "It's a promise of all the wonderful things to come."

They made it as far as the stairs before he had to stop and kiss her again. One thing led to another, and by the time they'd finished dallying, they'd both lost their boots. And jeans. Their shirts came off midway up the stairs, and their socks were strewn in the hall.

By the time they reached his bed, they were laughing, and

ready for more. "I knew I'd get these off eventually," he teased, relieving her of her bra and panties.

"I'm not the only one who is going to be naked." Emily divested Dylan of his boxer briefs.

Erotic moments passed as they each looked their fill.

"You are so beautiful," he whispered.

And aroused, she thought as she regarded him in the shadowy light of dusk. "You're pretty incredible, too," Emily said, taut and aching to be touched.

"So where do you want to start?" Dylan asked, trailing a hand down her hip. He kissed her shoulder, moved to her collarbone, then the tip of her breast.

Emily knew there was no reason to rush, no need to deny the feelings swirling around in her heart, no reason to worry about tomorrow. The last of her inhibitions melted away; she was in over her head and sinking fast. She reached for him wantonly and drew him toward the bed. "Wherever you want as long as we do everything you want and then some."

"Sounds like a plan," he rasped playfully, tumbling her down onto the sheets.

The next thing she knew they were lying on their sides. Emily closed her eyes as he kissed her lazily and worked his way up her thighs. His palms found her as her hands found him. They kissed and caressed until their whole bodies were melting against each other in boneless pleasure.

"Now," she murmured.

He shifted so she was beneath him.

Then slid lower still.

This wasn't what she meant…but it turned out to be exactly what she needed.

Emily went catapulting over the edge.

Dylan slid between her thighs and surged against her. Emily moaned in response. She wrapped her arms around him and brought her legs up so they were locked around his waist.

Dylan wanted to pretend the two of them weren't meant to be together, long-term, that this closeness would suffice. But he knew it wasn't true, that the promises they had made to each other, to let go and move on when the time was right, were vows they were not going to be able to keep.

Maybe she didn't love him, maybe she never would, but when they were together like this it felt as if they belonged together. And in this instance, Dylan knew, belonging together was enough.

IT WAS LATE MORNING, when Emily finally awakened to see Dylan stroll into the bedroom, tray in hand. She struggled to a sitting position, unable to help but think how good it felt to be together like this.

Dylan winked as their eyes met. "Since you have the day off…"

Emily moved her eyebrows teasingly in return, murmuring, "Thank heavens for small miracles." And it did seem like a miracle to be here with Dylan, at his ranch, after a wonderfully exciting and satisfying night of lovemaking. *And* have him bring her breakfast in bed! How had she gotten so lucky? Emily wasn't used to getting what she wanted in the romance department.

Usually, it was anything but.

And that made her uncertain…despite telling herself that given all that had happened recently, she had no reason to be.

Dylan waited for her to adjust the pillows behind her, then set the tray across her lap. "Are you going to be able to hang out here with me today?"

Emily smiled. "I was thinking I could help you with the horses. Maybe bring my mare Maisy over, and have Hercules, you and me all go for a ride."

"Sounds good. After you ride Ginger, that is."

Emily paused. "*Really* ride her?"

"I've worked with her a little more. I think she's ready for it now. The question is, are you?"

Was he kidding? "Wait and see."

An hour later, Emily was out in the round pen. Dylan brought Ginger in on a lead.

They started the session the way they always did, using the long cloth line to drive Ginger away. Emily constantly moved into Ginger's space, pressuring her at the flanks, gently yet firmly herding her forward.

Finally, when Ginger's head was level, her body nice and relaxed, Emily turned ninety degrees, offering her shoulder. She kept her head down, her body relaxed. As always, Ginger turned and came back toward Emily. She kept walking, quietly praising Ginger all the while.

The mare came closer still.

Lowered her head, bowed to Emily in respect.

Dylan, watching from center of the paddock, walked forward to hold her by the bridle. "I'll attach the reins. You put on the saddle."

Working like a well-practiced team, they readied the mustang. And this time, when Emily stepped up into the saddle, Ginger didn't only accept Emily's weight, she seemed to welcome it. She moved cautiously at first, then more and more boldly, until she was trotting around the pen.

From there, they went to a pasture, where a nice trot turned into a canter and then a full-fledged gallop around the perimeter.

When they had finished, Emily couldn't stop grinning.

"Congratulations on a job well done." Dylan gave her a high five. "We're well on our way to training her."

Emily beamed. "My family has got to see this!"

The minute the words were out, Emily knew she had made a mistake. Dylan didn't do family drama. Or meetings. Did that also mean he didn't do family parties? To her relief, whatever reservations he had quickly faded. "Of course your dad is going to want to see this," he said.

"My mom, too," Emily added, serious. "You can't really invite one without the other."

There was a brief hesitation, then Dylan gestured magnanimously. "Whenever you want," he said with a wide smile.

Taking this for the good sign it was, Emily said, "Tonight?"

Another hesitation, although briefer. Dylan nodded. "Call them right now."

Emily bounded off. "I will."

No sooner had Emily gotten off the phone with her parents than the phone rang again.

It was Simone. "You are not going to believe what is happening in Laramie right now!"

SHORT MINUTES LATER, Dylan and Emily stood side by side at her apartment window, watching the gas, electric and water be cut off to the site.

Xavier Shillingsworth was nowhere in sight during all this, and was still a no-show when the enormous crane moved forward to pick up the Cowtown Diner and lift it over onto the same double-wide tractor-trailer truck it had arrived on.

By late Sunday afternoon, the burnished bronze building was only a memory.

Emily turned to Dylan, "I can't believe they are moving out lock, stock and barrel, just like that."

Dylan couldn't, either. And yet, with the ongoing investigation closing in and legal action pending... "Customers here weren't going to go back. It was probably a good business decision to move the franchise restaurant to Big Springs."

Emily squinted. "I'm not sure he'll have any better luck there."

Dylan shrugged. "You never know. Shillingsworth might have learned something from all this."

Emily frowned. "One could hope."

"So about that little get-together at my ranch this evening..." Dylan interjected.

Emily's eyes lit up. "Seven o'clock okay? It shouldn't take long. All I'm going to do is give Ginger a few turns around the round pen for them."

Dylan found her enthusiasm contagious. "Take as long as you want. You deserve to show off for them."

She searched his face. "Would it be all right if I invited my brothers, too?"

Dylan knew if he was going to be part of Emily's life, he would have to get used to having her family around, too.

"The more, the merrier," he said.

Chapter Fourteen

"Looks like we're early," Shane McCabe said.

A good half hour early, Dylan noted, which wouldn't usually have been a problem. He could have easily entertained the horse rancher and his lovely wife, shown them around his property and had a good time doing it.

But that was before he'd begun sleeping with their only daughter.

Recalling his last conversation with Emily's dad, who had warned Dylan not to toy with Emily's feelings, Dylan ushered the couple inside his ranch house.

"Where should we put these?" Greta asked, indicating the four catering-size foil containers bearing her restaurant name.

Dylan relieved Greta of her burden and led the way.

What had started out as a brief horse-training demonstration for Emily's parents had turned into a potluck gathering for her entire family.

Dylan had no experience hosting a crowd. He usually went into town to socialize. He hoped he had enough plates and silverware. Or that someone had thought to bring disposable dinnerware. "I think the best place is the kitchen."

"I can put these in the oven for you, if you like," Greta offered.

There was a lot of Emily in her mom, and vice versa. Dylan smiled. "That'd be great. Thanks."

"So have you given any thought to the offer I made you?" Shane asked.

"I'm honored that you asked me to join forces with you in a nonprofit venture," he replied.

"But you're turning me down," Shane said with disappointment.

"I'd like to continue to train mustangs for you. I prefer to do it as an independent contractor."

Shane pressed, "We could do a lot of good if we founded a mustang sanctuary. We could take any wild horses that ranchers rounded up, train them and see they went to good homes."

"We can do that now without legally joining forces."

Shane studied Dylan for a long moment, and an awkward silence filled the room.

Greta moved to the window. "I think I heard another car," she said, slipping out.

"Is this because of my daughter?" Shane asked, up-front as ever.

As long as they were being candid… "Did you ask me because of your daughter? Because you were trying to somehow bring me into the fold?"

"McCabes don't just help family," Shane responded kindly. "They also help friends and neighbors."

Determined to learn the truth, Dylan said, "That's not really answering my question."

Shane folded his arms in front of him. "Are you involved with Emily, this pretend-dating business aside?"

Dylan hesitated. This was not a discussion he should be having with Emily's father until after he'd had it with Emily. "I don't know how to answer—"

"And you shouldn't have to," Emily interrupted.

Dylan and Shane turned in unison.

Dressed in jeans, boots and an embroidered turquoise shirt, she looked prettier than Dylan had ever seen her. Angrier, too.

Emily strode forward, blue eyes flashing. "I'm not a child, Dad."

Shane straightened, his need to protect his daughter unabated. "I never said you were."

Emily stabbed the air with her finger. "Every action you, mom and my brothers take says you all think I need protecting."

"Honey, you're our only daughter," Greta cut in.

"I'm a grown woman." Emily stood next to Dylan and linked arms with him. "And I deserve one heck of a lot more respect than you are showing me right now."

Before anyone else could say anything, Jeb and Holden appeared in the doorway. "Hey, sis!" Jeb said jubilantly. "When are we going to see the amazing demonstration?"

Her cheeks still pink with indignation, Emily muttered, "As soon as everyone is here."

As if on cue, the doorbell rang. More McCabes arrived, along with Andrew and Simone and Bobbie Sue and Billy Ray. The commotion in the kitchen increased as everyone brought their dinner contributions into the house.

Happy to have the tense family drama between Emily and her parents cut short, Dylan escaped the calamity and headed off to get the mustangs ready.

When Emily came out to the barns, with her gaggle of devotees streaming out around her, her mind seemed solely on the task ahead. Dylan forced himself to do the same.

Ginger, Salt and Pepper all performed as admirably as Dylan and Emily had hoped. The two younger horses—who were not big or strong enough to be ridden yet—went through their training exercises with ease.

Emily was clearly ecstatic. As was Dylan.

She ended the demonstration of the three-year-old mare's prowess with a solo canter around the pasture.

Dylan was as proud of Emily—and the work she had done—as he was of the horses. And he wasn't the only one. Her family whistled, clapped and shouted their approval as she came back to dismount and take her bows. For the first time, Dylan began to understand the allure of being a McCabe. The support they offered, the expression of love was unbelievable.

"So what's next?" Jeb asked.

"We test them to see if they've bonded to us—become part of our ranch family—as much as it appears they have," Dylan explained.

Further questions were cut off as another car sped up the lane and stopped short of them. Dylan swore as the male behind the wheel cut the engine and got out. This was exactly what they did not need.

EMILY KNEW it was Dylan's ranch, but Xavier was only there because of her. She put up a hand before Dylan could intervene.

"I'll take care of this." She handed off Ginger's reins to Jeb and she walked toward the interloper. Silence fell.

Shillingsworth handed her a thick manila envelope.

"A parting gift." Xavier smirked as if he still held the high card.

Knowing forewarned was forearmed, Emily took it reluctantly and undid the clasp. Inside was a thick folder bearing the name of a private investigator. "What is this?" she snapped.

He stared at her, his expression ugly. "A complete dossier on your friend there."

Emily stiffened. "I already know all about Dylan." *At least the parts that are important...*

Xavier gestured expansively and said even louder, "Then you also know he is one of the Texas Reeves. The railroad tycoon."

Emily turned to Dylan. On the surface, his expression was as inscrutable as usual. In his eyes, she could see a burning anger.

"Normally, that'd be a good thing." Xavier spoke to the crowd as if lecturing a class. "If the family acknowledged him, that was. Unfortunately, they do not."

Aware the ranch yard was so silent you could hear a pin drop, Xavier rubbed his jaw and continued. "I couldn't understand it until I went to see his grandfather myself." He shook his head. "You ought to see the fabulous mansion they live in. Anyway, I told the old man all about Dylan—where he was living, what he was doing, that he was trying to work his way into the famous McCabes by romancing one of their daughters."

Emily broke in pointedly. "That sounds more like your plan."

Xavier ignored her. "The old man didn't care. He said that it didn't matter who Dylan eventually married. Dylan was always going to have his father's white-trash blood, and that to hear about his grandson only reminded the old man of the way his own daughter ruined the family name by giving birth to a bastard that was no better than the lowlife that sired him—"

Emily didn't know where it came from. She had never been violent in her life. But suddenly the file folder was dropping to the ground and her hand was flying through the air.

Her fist connected with Xavier's jaw. To her disappointment, she didn't seem to hurt the obnoxious spoilsport a bit.

She did shut him up momentarily, however, as everyone stared on in shock.

It was then that Dylan stepped in, cool, calm and collected as ever.

"Emily, why don't you take everyone inside?" Dylan suggested, a dangerously civil edge to his low tone. "I'll escort this *gentleman* to his car."

Equally tense and irritable looks were exchanged all around. Evidently confident Dylan could handle it, they all complied with Dylan's request.

Only Emily remained.

Dylan looked at her. "Go inside, Emily," he repeated.

Dylan hadn't talked to her in that unwelcoming a tone since the first day she had shown up, asking him to pretend to be her date for the evening. Her lips parted in shock.

Xavier grinned triumphantly, pleased at the rancor his unexpected appearance had created.

"Right now," Dylan commanded.

Emily didn't want to leave, his tone brooked no argument. Heart pounding, spirits sinking, she turned on her heel and stomped off.

"YOU'RE NOT good enough for her."

Dylan picked up the papers and shoved them into Shillingsworth's hands. "So you said, several times."

Ignoring the danger he was in, Shillingsworth thrust out his jaw pugnaciously. "Her family may try to bring you into the fold, but at the end of the day, everyone knows you can't make a silk purse out of a sow's ear, and they'll cut you loose, too—the same way your biological family severed ties."

Dylan wanted to say the McCabes weren't like that.

He knew different.

They loved their daughter and wanted only the best for her.

They wanted all the things he didn't know how to give her. Like the foundation—through generations of example—for a good solid marriage and a happy family.

A husband who had a background she could be as proud of as her own.

As much as it pained Dylan to admit it, that wasn't him. Never had been. Never would be.

Shillingsworth continued his last hurrah. "One of these days soon, she'll realize she's made a mistake hooking up with you at all. When that happens, she'll dump you flat, buddy."

Not if we part amicably, Dylan thought, determined to protect Emily in whatever way remained. Unimpressed, he lifted a brow. "I doubt she'll come running to you."

Shillingsworth shrugged, apparently having finally let go of that particular fantasy. "That much I figured. Which is too bad. Emily missed out on a good thing with me—I could have shown her the world. Because I am not just a trust-fund baby whose money will eventually run out. I'm going to be filthy rich one day, all on my own."

"I'm sure they'll make a movie about you," Dylan returned dryly.

"They will! And I'll have all the women I want!"

"Good luck with that," he retorted.

"Just not here in this one-horse town."

His patience exhausted, Dylan propelled the kid into the driver's seat and shut the door. "You better get started, then. Time's a-wastin'."

"Don't I know it!" Shillingsworth released an obnoxious laugh, coupled with an invective-laced adios, and sped off.

Dylan could tell Shillingsworth was finally satisfied he'd gotten his revenge on both Emily and Dylan. The residents of Laramie would never see the kid again unless legal action dragged him back.

He turned to see Emily coming up behind him.

Her cheeks were pink with indignation, her eyes full of worry. "What did he say to you just now?"

Wishing things were different, Dylan exhaled. "The same thing he's been alleging all along, that I'm not good enough for you."

Emily recoiled with hurt. "That's not true."

Wasn't it? Dylan had seen the looks on all the McCabes' faces when Shillingsworth was describing his conversation with the old man. They'd been as shocked and revolted by the coldhearted account as Dylan would have expected them to be.

There was no way they'd want their daughter to be exposed to such familial disdain and cruelty, even by marriage.

Dylan swallowed and forced himself to do the right thing. To finally be as noble as he should have been all along.

He shrugged, keeping his tone carefully matter-of-fact. "Not that it matters. We knew this was only a temporary thing anyway, right?" He paused to search her eyes, protecting Emily the best way he could.

"Well. I—" she stammered, but he cut her off.

"Emily, let's not dance around the truth, okay?" he muttered. "It was always understood that we'd eventually go our separate ways."

Emily blinked. "But what about the mustangs…the test you talked about…?"

Dylan had inadvertently put her through so much; he wouldn't rob her of that. "You're welcome to participate in that, of course," he reassured her.

Emily's lower lip trembled. "When are you going to do it?" she whispered.

Dylan pushed away the powerful feelings welling up inside him. "In ten days or so. I'll let you know when I set it up."

"Dylan…"

He cut her off with a gallant lift of his hand. "We have

guests, Emily." It was all he could do not to wrap his arms around her. "Don't you think it's time you went to see about taking care of them?"

A flush started in her neck and swept into her face. Looking near tears, she asked hoarsely, "Don't you want to come inside, too?"

Dylan figured he had embarrassed her enough. "I'm going to see to the horses—get them settled for the night."

Aware they were no doubt being observed by the whole McCabe contingent, Emily struggled to regain her composure. "All right, then. I'll see you in a bit." She went back in to oversee the potluck dinner.

Dylan exited the ranch and left Emily to say goodbye to everyone on her own. He felt sick inside, but he knew he'd done the right thing. Because Shillingsworth was right—it would never work. Had he and Emily been smarter and more honest, they would have realized that from the very beginning.

Chapter Fifteen

Dylan was in the stable late the following afternoon when he heard a car motor. He walked out to see Andrew waving goodbye to his mom. "You're not scheduled to work today."

The teen walked slowly toward him, hands thrust in the pockets of his jeans. "I thought you might need some help with the mustangs. Emily not being here and all…"

As if Dylan needed reminding about that.

In the past twenty-two hours, all he'd done was think about her and wish things had been different. But they weren't… and he needed to remember that.

He motioned for Andrew to follow him. "How is Emily?"

Andrew plucked the leather work gloves from his back pocket and hurried to catch up. "She's real busy."

Dylan had tried to stay focused on other things, too. For once, concentrating on the needs of the horses in his care did nothing to stanch the overwhelming emotions welling up inside him. He stalked into the barn and picked up a fresh bale of hay, handed another off to Andrew. "I saw a Closed sign on the café when I drove into town today."

"She's taking the whole week off."

Another sign that things weren't right with her, either, although in her case her actions could all be financially motivated. "How come?" Dylan stopped to get a pair of clippers to cut the twine.

They both carried the hay into the stable and set it down in the center aisleway. "Well, today, anyway, she's busy meeting with the three guys her brothers brought in to talk to her. And then about five others are coming in, too."

Dylan felt a surge of possessiveness that was no longer justifiable. Telling himself his interest was only cursory, that if she were selling shares in her business or looking for outside investors he might be interested, too, Dylan asked casually, "All at the same time?"

Andrew helped break the two bales into equal flakes. "No. One after the other. Emily's real serious about it. She says the meetings all have to be private."

Okay, that could mean anything....

Andrew and Dylan stuffed the hay nets with feed. "Emily says she has to concentrate on her future now more than ever—and she wants to get things taken care of as soon as possible. That's all I know."

Dylan weighed the nets on a spring balance, to ensure the proper level of feed for each horse. Then he and Andrew brought them to the individual stalls and secured them at eye level on the wall.

Andrew grabbed a broom to clean up any leftover bits of hay that had fallen to the floor. Dylan studied the lingering concern on the boy's face.

"Is that the only reason you came out here?" Dylan asked as they walked out of the stable. "To tell me that?"

Andrew drifted toward the pasture fence. He looked toward the far corner, where Ginger, Salt and Pepper congregated in a corner, basking in the late-afternoon sun and the gentle spring breeze.

Andrew hooked his arms over the fence rail. He kept his gaze trained forward. "Actually, I wanted to ask you about the stuff Xavier Shillingsworth said about you being from a not-so-nice family."

Dylan knew how difficult it was for the fifteen-year-old to let anyone know what was really on his mind. "I imagine a lot of people want to ask me about that," he replied with as much candor as he could muster.

Andrew gulped and turned to Dylan. "Did it make you feel bad having him say all those things?" He squinted and turned his gaze to the horizon again. His hands gripped the rail in front of him. "'Cause it always makes me feel bad when people talk about my dad being arrested and being sent to jail."

Dylan started to say the expected—that it didn't matter what others thought and therefore he refused to let it bother him. But he knew that wasn't true.

"It hurts," he said finally, deciding to go outside his comfort zone and give the troubled teen the uncensored honesty he deserved. "It makes me feel I'm being blamed for something outside my control."

Andrew shifted again and braced his body against the rail. "Does it make you mad?"

"It used to—now I just find it kind of sad and discouraging. And, of course, unfair."

Andrew clenched his jaw. "Some parents think because my dad did bad things, and I have his blood, that I'll do bad things. So they don't want me being friends with their kids or asking their daughters out on dates."

Dylan hadn't known that was happening. He was pretty sure Simone and Emily hadn't, either.

Andrew hastened to add, "Most of the kids are okay— they'd like to hang out with me but they're just not allowed to. Only the kids who have parents who don't care what their kids do—"

"Kids who are already in trouble of some sort," Dylan interjected, guessing the rest.

Andrew nodded. "Those kids are always allowed to go places with me. No problem."

Which explained, Dylan thought, Andrew's entry into a bad crowd shortly after moving to Laramie. It wasn't because he had wanted to be part of that group; he hadn't felt he had any other options. "Did you ever tell your mom this?"

Andrew hung his head. "I didn't see the point. She feels bad enough about the stuff my dad did, and the trouble it caused for us back in Houston. We had to pack up and start over someplace else. I didn't want to make it worse for her. But at the same time," Andrew continued in a rusty-sounding voice, "it can get really lonely, when you don't have any other kids to go places with who aren't going to get you in trouble again."

"Yes," Dylan said, knowing from his own experiences that was the case. "It can. But it doesn't have to stay that way, Andrew. Now that we know what the situation is, I can vouch for you with other parents." He put a reassuring hand on Andrew's shoulder. "So if you need a reference, you have them call me. I'll assure the other parents that you are a good influence for their kids."

"You'd do that for me?"

"I gave you a community-service job on the ranch, didn't I? I'm teaching you how to care for horses. Of course I'll do that for you."

Andrew grinned his relief. "I didn't think anyone would understand. But then, I guess you know all about this kind of stuff. Because your background isn't considered great, either. Since you were disowned at birth and several times since."

Dylan winced. *Gee, when you put it like that...*

Andrew's brows drew together. "Is that why you and Emily broke up?" he blurted out, perplexed. "Because she found out that you don't have the kind of family she does and now she doesn't want to go out with you anymore? Are you being discriminated against, too?"

Dylan held up a staying hand. "Emily's not like that."

She was the kind of woman who made him believe in happily-ever-after, who made him want the fairy tale for himself.

Andrew frowned, still not getting it. "Then why did you leave the party like that last night, without saying goodbye to anyone?" he demanded.

Easy, Dylan thought. Because she's a wonderful woman who deserves to see all her dreams come true. And those dreams included being with a man who understood how to be part of a big, happy family, a man who knew instinctively what to do and say and belong. Instead of someone who was always waiting for the other shoe to drop.

Fighting the turbulent emotions, Dylan cleared his throat. He looked at Andrew, man to man. "I didn't come back to the ranch house last night as I figured Emily had been embarrassed enough. I couldn't see doing it to her over and over again in the future. Because all of that will come up."

"My background will come up, too. But you're willing to be my friend and vouch for me."

"That's different," Dylan retorted.

"How?" the teen persisted.

"It's complicated," he said finally.

Andrew scoffed. "When adults say that it usually means they're in love or something."

"*Or something* being the operative words in this case," Dylan said.

Had he and Emily not promised to keep it casual, to never change, to part amicably before things got convoluted and messy?

"Yeah, well," Andrew grumbled, as the trio of mustangs saw them and started their way, "as long as we're talking straight to each other… I gotta say, I think you humiliated

Emily more by leaving the party that way, without even saying good night to anybody or anything."

Guilt wound its way into his heart. And stayed. He'd figured he had been helping, by exiting quietly and unobtrusively, instead of staying and being the elephant in the room. "Did she say that?" he demanded, his mouth dry.

Or was this Andrew misinterpreting?

Andrew looked at Dylan as if he was an idiot. "Emily didn't have to complain about it. My mom and I could both see she was really hurt." Andrew stopped and shook his head. "You really ought to go to her and apologize. Try and do something to make it right."

EMILY HAD just shut off the café coffeemaker and was getting ready to clean up, when her mother walked in. Emily knew she was concerned and that she'd show up eventually to talk to her.

"Full calendar today, hmm?" Greta started sympathetically. She opened up the bag she'd brought with her. Inside were two pints of premium ice cream—Godiva chocolate for Emily, coconut-pecan for her mother.

Emily accepted the gift with a thank you and found two spoons. "I decided to finally start tackling the café's problems head-on. I actually got a lot of offers of help, some very interesting."

As comfortable in a commercial kitchen as she was in her own home, Greta pulled up a stool to the central worktable. "Are there any you are going to accept?"

Emily brought two glasses of ice water over to the table. "Yes. I've already set up time to meet with five of them again."

Greta smiled. "That's great."

Emily savored her first bite of dark-chocolate ice cream. "But that's not why you came over to talk to me."

"Your father and I are both concerned about Dylan."

Pushing aside the memory of the sexy rancher, and all he had once meant to her, Emily savored another bite. Like it or not, she had to move on in this regard, too. "I can't help you."

Greta studied her carefully. "You're no longer friends?"

No longer friends with temporary benefits, that was for sure, Emily thought miserably, wondering how something that had felt so right could go so wrong so fast.

"Our reasons for seeing each other are over." Knowing she had to unburden herself to someone, she said, "I know we put on a good show from time to time, Mom, but it was all just pretend."

A twinkle appeared in Greta's eyes. "Really."

Now was not the time for her mother to get overly romantic in her outlook. *"Really,"* she reiterated.

Greta sipped her ice water. "What about the feelings in your heart? Are those pretend, too?"

Emily flushed. "It doesn't matter. Dylan's right…he's never going to be the guy I need."

I need someone who wants me, for now, for always. Someone who is willing to negotiate and adapt, grow old with me…

"Because he's not ethical."

Where had her mother gotten that idea? "He's ethical!"

Greta's elegant eyebrows furrowed. "Not strong willed enough to take you on, then?"

Emily choked in exasperation. "Have you met the man?"

Greta savored another bite. "I guess, then, he's lacking a tender side."

This, Emily thought, was beginning to get annoying. "Have you forgotten he's a horse whisperer? Honestly, Mom, Dylan is the most gentle, intuitive man I have ever met in my entire life." He knew how to kiss her and touch her and hold her. When to talk, and when to just let her be...

Greta wrinkled her nose, thinking. "Then it's his background."

There was no doubt about it—most of his family life had been heartbreakingly sad. "He can't get over the cruelness of the rejection. And to have it happen again, last night, through Xavier, in front of everyone in our family." It had been a nightmare, and not for just him.

"It is a lot to have to accept," Greta remarked quietly. "Especially when he is so deserving."

Emily set down her spoon. "You know what the worst part of it was?" Her mom shook her head, listening. "The fact that I couldn't help him and be the kind of life partner he needed when it actually happened. I wanted to help him. I wanted to do or say something to make it all better for him, but in that moment, I didn't have a clue."

"You stood up for him. You made the first move to send Xavier on his way."

"That was easy, Mom. I'm a McCabe—I know how to stand up for family. But I didn't know how to handle the rest of it or what to say to him that would have made it all okay. Instead, when put to the test, I faltered, and he...left."

"That doesn't mean the two of you have to break off your whatever it is you've been having."

What had they been having? An affair? Or something a heck of a lot more?

"Unless you're angry with him."

"I'm disappointed," Emily admitted miserably.

"Why?"

"Because I kind of feel he lumped me in with everyone else who has let him down. He didn't give me a chance to grow and learn and do better. And be what he needs. I'm not like that. Instead, it was like, 'well...obviously this isn't going to work.'" Angry tears sprang to her eyes. "Like he expected that at any minute I would turn my back on him, because of his horribly callous relatives…so he called up this agreement we had made to end it at the first sign of trouble and dumped me first!"

Greta struggled to follow the logic. "So, if you had dumped *him* first it would have been okay?"

"*No!* The point is, I wouldn't have dumped him at all!"

"Isn't that what you're doing now?"

Emily fell abruptly silent.

She struggled to explain how something that had started out so simply—as a reckless and ill-thought-out ruse to avoid some matchmaking—had evolved into something so passionate and meaningful—and ultimately devastating, as well. "We had an agreement—" Emily struggled not to cry "—that we wouldn't try to change each other. The way I always tried to change the guys I dated. Dylan didn't want to be another fixer-upper for me.

"But did that also mean we shouldn't try on our own to change for the better?" She wondered fervently. "Because I thought that's what people in love did! I thought just being together made them better people. And that implies change, doesn't it?"

"Usually, unless the two people involved are absolutely perfect individuals to begin with," her mother replied. "And personally, I can't think of a single instance where that has happened."

"So he *is* being unreasonable!" Emily crowed, more hurt and angry than ever.

Greta released a gusty breath. "Look, Emily, I know you and your brothers are all grown. And I really do try and stay out of your love lives as much as possible."

Emily couldn't help it—she laughed out loud. *"Really?"*

she echoed, reacting to the audacity. "Because, several weeks ago I heard you were trying to set me up with some mystery guy that you thought would be just perfect for me."

Greta looked chagrined they were suddenly back to that. "Your brothers told you," she murmured, actually blushing.

Emily threw up her hands in exasperation. "They're my sibs! Of course they warned me!" She aimed a censuring finger her mother's way. "The only one who didn't tell me about The Guy Who Might Be The One For Me was you. *You* backed off before ever uttering his name!"

Greta replaced the top on her ice cream. "There was a reason for that," she said, rising to her feet.

"And it was?" Emily stood, too.

The self-conscious pink in her mother's cheeks deepened. She cleared her throat as if making a grand announcement. "You were already kissing him at the time." Greta paused to let the weight of her words sink in. "Frankly, your father and I concluded we didn't *need* to do anything else to get you to give the guy a second look."

Emily's mouth dropped open. "You really wanted me to be with Dylan?"

Her mother was firm. "We really did."

Wow. And Wow again. "And now?" Emily ventured at last.

Greta grabbed her purse. "Honey, that's up to you. We'll back you in whatever you decide." She resacked her half-finished pint and headed for the door.

A still-reeling Emily followed close behind, aware for the first time in hours her heart held a smidgen of hope. "But…"

Her mother turned before going out the door. "Nope. No more advice," she reiterated firmly, looking Emily straight in the eye. The air reverberated with maternal and familial love.

"Because the wisdom you need—" Greta took Emily's hand and placed it over her daughter's heart "—is already *right in here.*"

EMILY TOOK her mother's advice and spent the next week searching her soul for the answers. Her chance to put her feelings to the test came a few days after that, when she met Dylan at a private mustang preserve 130 miles from the Last Chance Ranch.

By the time she arrived, ready to witness the wild horses' first big test, he was already there, unloading the three mustangs and his own gelding from the four-horse trailer. The youngest two were outfitted with reins and lead lines; the older two horses were saddled up.

Emily got out of the Circle M pickup truck she had borrowed from her father and walked over to join the group. In the distance, they could see the resident herd of mustangs, grazing sedately in the 100-acre preserve.

But it was the man next to her that held her heart captive.

It had only been a week and a half, yet as Emily looked into those familiar golden-brown eyes, it felt so much longer. Too long.

She swallowed, trying not to notice how handsome he looked, with his hat tugged low over his brow, a new haircut and a fresh shave. Or how good he smelled, like sandalwood and leather and soap.

"Tell me again how this is going to work," Emily said.

His eyes were alight with kindness and another emotion she couldn't identify. "We're going to lead the horses a little closer, and then dismount and let the mustangs go." He flexed his broad shoulders lazily. "See what they do, given the choice."

"Well, of course they're going to race off to be with the other mustangs," Emily said in frustration. Horses were herd animals, after all. Unlike humans, they always chose to be with their kind over being alone.

He gave her a brief, officious look. "I reckon that's so."

Emily's anxiety rose. "It doesn't bother you?"

Dylan adjusted the stirrups on Ginger's saddle. "If they've bonded, the way we think they have, and become part of the Last Chance Ranch family, they won't stay away from us for very long," he explained.

"And if they haven't?"

Dylan offered Emily a hand up into Ginger's saddle. As soon as she was situated, he climbed onto Hercules's back. "Then they'll likely never make reliable domesticated riding horses." He frowned. "They'll always be looking to run off, first chance they get, and they wouldn't be suitable for the boys ranch."

He reined in Salt and Pepper, and they headed off at an easy canter. They stopped again, atop the hill overlooking the pasture. Ginger was already prancing around in excitement. Salt and Pepper followed suit. Only Hercules, Dylan's well-trained gelding, remained calm and almost uninterested.

Dylan climbed down and tied his horse to a tree.

Emily dismounted, too. Together, they removed Ginger's saddle, all three mustangs' bridles and bits and stepped away.

The moment Ginger realized she was free, she turned back, gave them one last look, then reared around and took off. Salt and Pepper followed her, both going at top speed, too.

Emily stood, boots planted firmly in the grass, arms folded in front of her, watching. Would they stay or come back? she wondered, her heart pounding.

Within her, there was so much sadness and disappointment. She knew now it was foolish, but she wished Dylan had given her the slightest sign. She'd really thought she and Dylan were going to be the ones riding off into the sunset together, that they'd spend the rest of their lives training and caring for mustangs in need of a good home.

Instead, here they were, acting as if they'd never been anything more than the most casual of friends. Acting as if their lovemaking…the long intimate talks…the joy they'd felt when together…hadn't mattered.

Here they were, about to say a final goodbye to each other, too, as they watched the three mustangs join the herd—without a thought as to the possibilities they were leaving behind. Tears blurring her eyes, unable to stand seeing any more, she turned and began walking away.

"Emily," Dylan rasped.

Emily could hear him behind her, gaining ground.

She rushed on, feeling as if her heart was breaking. What had made her think she could handle any of this, she wondered, as she dabbed at the moisture flooding her eyes.

She wasn't strong enough to love and let go.

She didn't want to forge on alone.

Yet that was the only choice she had.

"Emily!" Dylan caught her by the shoulders and spun her around to face him.

Fifty yards away, Hercules chewed grass sedately. As if all was right with the world…

"What?" Emily snapped.

Dylan looked just as impatient. "Why are you crying?"

Emily sniffed. She'd never thought Dylan insensitive—until now. "Why aren't *you?*"

He seemed puzzled. "We don't know yet what they're going to do."

Emily cast a look at the mustangs they'd just let go—now romping with the herd of wild horses. "I think it's pretty clear." They were leaving her, just as Dylan had left her.

He frowned, nowhere near ready to give up. "They're exploring their options."

Emily harrumphed. That sounded like a line and a half!

Dylan surprised her by saying, "Kind of like you and that long line of guys you were interviewing at the café the other day?"

Was the rough note in his voice possessiveness? Emily tensed and folded her arms in front of her. "How did you know about that?"

Dylan's eyes darkened. "Andrew might have mentioned it."

The silence strung out between them.

"So I guess you're back to dating," he said deferentially.

Emily adopted his businesslike attitude. "I'm back to saving my café. I've decided to respond to customer demand and expand."

His face relaxed and he moved closer still. "The tables outside aren't enough?"

Emily basked in his nearness. "No." She pressed her lips together. "And as we've already proved, they aren't available in inclement weather, either. I've applied for permits to put in an elevator and make my apartment over the shop into a second dining area and a separate party room." She smiled in triumph. "It looks like I'm going to get it, too."

He stroked his jaw. "So the guys…"

"Were all volunteering to help me in one way or another. Construction will start right away. I'm going to pay them in meal vouchers."

"That's a great idea."

"Thanks," she said.

He sobered, every inch of him resolute male. "Where are you going to live in the meantime?"

Finally, a problem she hadn't had time to solve. Emily bit her lip. "I don't know yet. Everyone in the family has offered to put me up for the duration, until I can afford another place, but…"

"Too much interference?" he guessed.

"Too many questions I don't want to answer." *Don't know how to answer.*

He took her hand in his and squeezed it tightly. "If you're looking for a roommate—" he looked her right in the eye "—I volunteer my place."

THIS WAS WHAT she wanted, Emily thought. And yet… She put up a palm to keep him from coming any nearer. "I can't go back to that, Dylan. To thinking only about the moment we're in, never knowing what tomorrow is going to bring." She cleared her throat. "Freedom is important, but…"

He came closer anyway, wrapping an arm about her waist. When she would have drawn away, he held fast. "You want more than that." His voice was a sexy rumble in his chest.

Emily drew a stabilizing breath and forced herself to be completely honest. "I need more than that, Dylan. I need to belong with someone, not just for right now, but for the rest of our lives." Trying not to notice how warm and solid and right he felt, she splayed her hands across his chest. Her voice trembled as she admitted, "I need permanence and security and family."

"Suppose I could give you that happily-ever-after?" he propositioned huskily.

She blinked back a mist of emotion, and reminded him, "You don't do family drama, remember?"

"I didn't used to—until I hooked up with you."

Ignoring the sudden wobbliness of her knees, Emily tried to figure out where this was going. "What are you talking about?" she asked, acknowledging the sudden reckless beat of her heart.

He tightened his grip on her, and said thoughtfully, "I had a talk with your dad."

"I know. You turned down his offer to go into business together."

"Not that conversation." His lips curved into a sexy smile. "Another one," he told her softly, gazing into her eyes. "I spoke to him yesterday and asked his permission."

A shiver swept through her. Aware how close she was to breathlessly surrendering to Dylan on any terms, she drew back and regarded him sternly. "This isn't funny."

"It's not supposed to be." He continued to search her face. "It's supposed to be romantic." He let the words sink in, then flashed the impish grin she loved so much. "And by the way?" he explained. "Your dad said okay."

Her parents *had* always wanted her to be happy. "You seem surprised by that," she noted, coming closer once again.

Sorrow mingled with joy on his handsome face. "I wasn't sure your family would think I was good enough for you." He swallowed, then began to relax. "Apparently, I am."

And suddenly, Emily and Dylan were right back where they had started. With her family calling the shots—or trying to—where her love life was concerned.

Tears of exasperation blurred her vision. She knew that if she and Dylan were ever to be happy, there were a few things they had to clear up first.

She stepped back, throwing up her hands in aggravation. "What is it with me that I keep getting these half measures?"

Dylan blinked. Apparently, she thought temperamentally, *this* hadn't been in his plan.

"What's *half measure* about me asking your father for your hand in marriage?" he demanded right back.

No longer sure who was taming who, or even who *should* be taming who, she retorted, "Gee, Dylan, I don't know. Maybe the fact that I kind of like to make those types of great big life-altering decisions for myself?"

Dylan narrowed his eyes. "You want me to ask you first?"

"For heaven's sake! Yes, I want you to ask me and not anyone else!" Emily blurted out her feelings before she could stop herself.

With a grin as wide as Texas, and a sparkle in his eyes, Dylan got down on his knees. He swept off his hat, set it against his chest and tilted his face up to hers. He was, at that moment, the epitome of masculine sexiness.

A few days ago, Emily would have happily succumbed. She would have thrust herself into his arms and kissed him wildly and let him kiss her back, and then let that lead where they both knew it would—to a hot session in bed.

Not anymore.

Not with all there was at stake.

She glared at him, waiting to see just how deep and real his commitment to her truly was. Because without that…

"Emily." His smile broadened all the more. "Will you marry me?"

She tugged on his hands and pulled him upright so they were squaring off—cowgirl to cowboy—once again.

"Why?" she demanded, aware the wrong rationale would not only break her heart, it would destroy them forever.

But this once, Dylan let down his guard and didn't disappoint. He wrapped his arms about her waist and regarded her with all the tenderness and affection she had always wished for.

"Because I love you, Emily," he said softly, looking deep into her eyes, with a tenderness that took her breath away.

"I love you the way I never thought I could love anyone. The way I'll never love anyone again." His voice caught. He forged on, the words coming from deep in his soul. "And because you're a part of my heart now, and I'll never be happy without you."

Emily's lower lip trembled. "I'll never be happy without you, either. And I love you, too, Dylan, so very much."

Relieved to finally be able to admit what was in her heart, Emily went up on tiptoe and kissed Dylan with every bit of the passion and love she felt. She kissed him until the moment became real, the romantic aura around them stunning in its power and intensity. And then she kissed him some more and let him kiss her back. Knowing what had started out as a temporary liaison wasn't temporary at all.

Finally, Dylan unlocked their lips and drew back just far enough to ask, "So...about my proposal?"

Emily cuddled close, still free-thinking and independent enough to insist, "It's yes to the roommate, no to the marriage."

He arched his eyebrow.

Practically, she explained, "I want us to live together first."

It was Dylan's turn to be wary. "That's not very traditional."

"So?"

"Your family isn't going to like that," he warned.

"It's not my family's decision—it's ours. And I want us to work things out in our own time and our own way, without anyone in my family pushing us to the altar." She met his eyes. "So what do you say? You...me...and the freedom to pursue everything and anything we've ever wanted?"

Emily felt a whisper of breath behind her. A very hot, gusty breath.

She turned, came face-to-face with a stealthily moving Ginger. Salt and Pepper were coming up right beside the mare.

Joy flowed through her as Ginger hooked her face over Emily's shoulder, in the equine version of a horse-to-human hug, then reached over and affectionately nosed Dylan's face and shoulder, too.

Emily laughed. "Well, what do you know, cowboy. I think our family's back."

Dylan chuckled, too. "And just in time," he stated, his eyes twinkling with happiness. "Because my answer to *your* proposal is yes!"

Epilogue

One year later...

"I can't believe we're doing this." Emily told Dylan as she took her place in Maisy's saddle, the voluminous folds of her white lace-and-satin wedding gown floating out about her.

Her groom-to-be grinned and climbed onto the magnificent Hercules. Resplendent in his tux, Dylan mugged at her seductively. "Yeah, you can."

Emily reached across and clasped his hand. She smiled, too. "Yeah. I can."

"It has been quite a year, though," he murmured.

Yes, Emily thought, it had.

They had secured proof linking Xavier Shillingsworth to the scandal in the cafe. An out-of-court settlement had been reached, both with her and the county health department, compensating them for their losses.

After that, her café had been remodeled in record time.

Emily'd had to scale back on the daily specials a bit in order to keep the books nicely balanced in the future, but thanks to an expanded, updated menu and additional seating, customer satisfaction was at an all-time high nevertheless.

Dylan had accepted her family into his heart as readily as they had taken him into theirs.

Andrew had plenty of friends and was now a ranch hand on

the Last Chance, working at Dylan's side whenever he wasn't in school or out socializing.

The only difficulty, if there was one, was the fact they'd had to take all three of the mustangs on to the Libertyville Boys Ranch, as promised.

Saying goodbye to the three beloved mustangs had been hard—until Emily saw how much the boys there loved horses, and how much Salt, Pepper and Ginger loved them back. She'd had to admit that the once-wild mustangs would have great lives as therapy horses.

And so now, it was on with the future. *Their* future, Emily thought, as Dylan stopped, atop a ridge. In the valley below, their family and friends waited.

He turned to her. "Before I give the signal for the musicians to start, I want to talk about the wedding gift."

He reached into his pocket and withdrew an envelope. Inside were photos of two beautiful mustangs.

Emily knew immediately what he had done. Entranced by the love of her life's generosity and acknowledging the unique challenges ahead—she asked, "When are they arriving?"

"The day after we get back from our honeymoon in Wyoming," Dylan reported proudly.

Emily chuckled. "And now my gift for you." She reached down and removed the envelope she had taped to the inside of her white satin cowgirl wedding boot.

She handed them over with a comical wrinkle of her nose. Dylan studied the photos—of two more mustangs—and began to laugh.

"Four mustangs," he said in awe.

Emily grinned, thinking how exciting it was going to be to start all over again. "Apparently."

Dylan slipped out of his saddle and pulled her out of hers. He wrapped his arms around her. "Think we can handle it?"

Emily wreathed her arms about his neck, rose on tiptoe and kissed him soundly. She looked deeply into his eyes. "Cowboy, I think we can handle anything as long as we're together."

Dylan murmured his agreement. He kissed her back leisurely. "So what do you say we ride on down there and get married?"

Emily hugged him with all the love in her heart. "I think that's the best idea ever," she beamed.

* * * * *

Watch for the next book in
Cathy Gillen Thacker's
TEXAS LEGACIES: THE MCCABES *Miniseries,*
HER COWBOY DADDY.
Only from Harlequin American Romance.

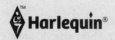

Harlequin®

COMING NEXT MONTH

Available May 10, 2011

#1353 A RANCHER'S PRIDE
American Romance's Men of the West
Barbara White Daille

#1354 THE COWBOY'S TRIPLETS
Callahan Cowboys
Tina Leonard

#1355 SUDDENLY TEXAN
Brody's Crossing
Victoria Chancellor

#1356 THE MARRIAGE SOLUTION
Fatherhood
Megan Kelly

You can find more information on upcoming
Harlequin® titles, free excerpts and more at
www.HarlequinInsideRomance.com.

HARCNM0411

REQUEST YOUR FREE BOOKS!
2 FREE NOVELS PLUS 2 FREE GIFTS!

Harlequin®

American ★ Romance®

LOVE, HOME & HAPPINESS

YES! Please send me 2 FREE Harlequin American Romance® novels and my 2 FREE gifts (gifts are worth about $10). After receiving them, if I don't wish to receive any more books, I can return the shipping statement marked "cancel." If I don't cancel, I will receive 4 brand-new novels every month and be billed just $4.24 per book in the U.S. or $4.99 per book in Canada. That's a saving of at least 15% off the cover price! It's quite a bargain! Shipping and handling is just 50¢ per book in the U.S. and 75¢ per book in Canada.* I understand that accepting the 2 free books and gifts places me under no obligation to buy anything. I can always return a shipment and cancel at any time. Even if I never buy another book, the two free books and gifts are mine to keep forever.

154/354 HDN FDKS

Name	(PLEASE PRINT)

Address	Apt. #

City	State/Prov.	Zip/Postal Code

Signature (if under 18, a parent or guardian must sign)

Mail to the **Reader Service:**
IN U.S.A.: P.O. Box 1867, Buffalo, NY 14240-1867
IN CANADA: P.O. Box 609, Fort Erie, Ontario L2A 5X3

Not valid for current subscribers to Harlequin American Romance books.

Want to try two free books from another line?
Call 1-800-873-8635 or visit www.ReaderService.com.

* Terms and prices subject to change without notice. Prices do not include applicable taxes. Sales tax applicable in N.Y. Canadian residents will be charged applicable taxes. Offer not valid in Quebec. This offer is limited to one order per household. All orders subject to credit approval. Credit or debit balances in a customer's account(s) may be offset by any other outstanding balance owed by or to the customer. Please allow 4 to 6 weeks for delivery. Offer available while quantities last.

Your Privacy—The Reader Service is committed to protecting your privacy. Our Privacy Policy is available online at www.ReaderService.com or upon request from the Reader Service.

We make a portion of our mailing list available to reputable third parties that offer products we believe may interest you. If you prefer that we not exchange your name with third parties, or if you wish to clarify or modify your communication preferences, please visit us at www.ReaderService.com/consumerschoice or write to us at Reader Service Preference Service, P.O. Box 9062, Buffalo, NY 14269. Include your complete name and address.

HAR11

*With an evil force hell-bent on destruction,
two enemies must unite to find a truth that turns
all-too-personal when passions collide.*

*Enjoy a sneak peek in Jenna Kernan's next installment
in her original* TRACKER *series, GHOST STALKER,
available in May, only from Harlequin Nocturne.*

"Who are you?" he snarled.

Jessie lifted her chin. "Your better."

His smile was cold. "Such arrogance could only come from a Niyanoka."

She nodded. "Why are you here?"

"I don't know." He glanced about her room. "I asked the birds to take me to a healer."

"And they have done so. Is that *all* you asked?"

"No. To lead them away from my friends." His eyes fluttered and she saw them roll over white.

Jessie straightened, preparing to flee, but he roused himself and mastered the momentary weakness. His eyes snapped open, locking on her.

Her heart hammered as she inched back.

"Lead who away?" she whispered, suddenly afraid of the answer.

"The ghosts. Nagi sent them to attack me so I would bring them to her."

The wolf must be deranged because Nagi did not send ghosts to attack living creatures. He captured the evil ones after their death if they refused to walk the Way of Souls, forcing them to face judgment.

"Her? The healer you seek is also female?"

"Michaela. She's Niyanoka, like you. The last Seer of Souls and Nagi wants her dead."

Jessie fell back to her seat on the carpet as the possibility of this ricocheted in her brain. Could it be true?

"Why should I believe you?" But she knew why. His black aura, the part that said he had been touched by death. Only a ghost could do that. But it made no sense.

Why would Nagi hunt one of her people and why would a Skinwalker want to protect her? She had been trained from birth to hate the Skinwalkers, to consider them a threat.

His intent blue eyes pinned her. Jessie felt her mouth go dry as she considered the impossible. Could the trickster be speaking the truth? Great Mystery, what evil was this?

She stared in astonishment. There was only one way to find her answers. But she had never even met a Skinwalker before and so did not even know if they dreamed.

But if he dreamed, she would have her chance to learn the truth.

Look for GHOST STALKER by Jenna Kernan, available May only from Harlequin Nocturne, wherever books and ebooks are sold.

Fan favorite author
TINA LEONARD
is back with
an exciting new miniseries.

Six bachelor brothers are given a challenge—
get married, start a big family and whoever does
so first will inherit the famed Rancho Diablo.
Too bad none of these cowboys is marriage material!

Callahan Cowboys:
Catch one if you can!

The Cowboy's Triplets (May 2011)
The Cowboy's Bonus Baby (July 2011)
The Bull Rider's Twins (Sept 2011)
Bonus Callahan Christmas Novella! (Nov 2011)
His Valentine Triplets (Jan 2012)
Cowboy Sam's Quadruplets (March 2012)
A Callahan Wedding (May 2012)

Harlequin® Romance

*Don't miss an irresistible new trilogy
from acclaimed author*

SUSAN MEIER

IN THE BOARDROOM

Greek Tycoons become devoted dads!

Coming in April 2011
The Baby Project

Whitney Ross is terrified when she becomes guardian
to a tiny baby boy, but everything changes when
she meets dashing Darius Andreas, Greek tycoon
and now a brand-new daddy!

Second Chance Baby (May 2011)
Baby on the Ranch (June 2011)

www.eHarlequin.com

HR17721

Love Inspired
HISTORICAL

INSPIRATIONAL HISTORICAL ROMANCE

*Introducing a brand-new
heartwarming Amish miniseries,*

AMISH BRIDES
of Celery Fields

Beginning in May with

Hannah's Journey

by ANNA SCHMIDT

Levi Harmon, a wealthy circus owner, never expected to find
the embodiment of all he wanted in the soft-spoken, plainly
dressed woman. And for the Amish widow Hannah Goodloe,
to love an outsider was to be shunned. The simple pleasures
of family, faith and a place to belong seemed an impossible
dream. Unless Levi unlocked his past and opened his heart
to God's plan.

*Find out if love can conquer all
in HANNAH'S JOURNEY,
available May wherever books are sold.*

www.LoveInspiredBooks.com

LIH82868